To the one who never knew

PRONAMI BORAH

ISBN
Paperback 979-8-89929-895-0
Hardcase 979-8-89961-301-2

Prologue

"Somewhere between the tea gardens and temple bells, I left pieces of myself—scattered like prayers on the wind. This story is a collection of them."

Contents

Contents

Chapter 1

The Day Love Took Shape

The house didn't just look beautiful — it felt alive.

Not in the ordinary sense, but in the way old homes do when they become vessels for memories in the making. Every wall echoed with laughter that had found its voice after months of waiting. The scent of fresh marigold and mogra swirled through the air, clinging to the soft folds of silk sarees and whispered secrets.

Light spilled into every corner — warm, golden, hopeful — filtering through sheer curtains that danced ever so slightly with the breeze. Strings of fairy lights blinked like stars come down to bless this very home. In one corner, a grandmother recited an old folk song. In another, giggles erupted over a lipstick shade gone wrong. It was messy. Loud. Raw. Real.

It was perfect!

And in the middle of all this lived a silence.

A sacred, trembling silence — the kind that exists only in the moments before something beautiful begins.

Upstairs, tucked away in a softly lit room, stood Pranavi. Her reflection shimmered in the mirror, but her eyes — lined with kohl and wonder — were elsewhere. Dressed in blush pink and draped in dreams, she held her phone close, the screen lighting up her anticipation. Her hands, still sticky with Mehendi, trembled as she pressed the call button.

The ringtone was painfully slow.

Then — a click.

Pranavi (excitedly, over a call):

"Hey!!! Where are you? I've been trying to reach you for the last ten minutes! I'm all set for our 'D' Day. I can't even describe how happy I am right now. I just… I want to thank you for everything, Ayush. You've given me the best gift ever by being you. Thank you for being such a wonderful part of my life. I couldn't have done any of this without you."

Far from the noise, beneath a canopy still being strung up with fresh flowers, Ayush stood in his sherwani — simple, elegant, and completely unaware of how stunning he looked in that moment. He leaned against an old pillar wrapped in fairy lights, watching the sky slowly give way to dusk.

He smiled the kind of smile you only wear once in a lifetime.

Ayush (with a smile in his voice):

"Pranavi, you have no idea how lucky I feel to have you. You've been my strongest support through everything, and I can't imagine my life without you. Today is not just your day or mine — it's our new beginning. Here's to us, and to all the love and madness ahead. Welcome to forever, Mrs. Ayush. ;)"

She giggled, that soft kind of laugh that bubbles up when your heart is just too full to keep quiet.

Pranavi (laughing softly):

"Mrs. Ayush... That sounds so surreal! Honestly, I'm a bundle of emotions right now—excited, nervous, overwhelmed, everything. I can't stop thinking about how far we've come, the challenges we've faced, and everything that's led to this moment. It's like... every memory, every tough day—it's all flashing before my eyes."

For a second, the chaos outside faded. There was only her voice. Her breath. Her heart, steadying itself.

Ayush (reassuringly):

"I know, love. It's natural to feel nostalgic, especially on a day as big as this. But remember, all those challenges made you who you are — the amazing, strong, and kind person I fell in love with. And guess what? You don't have to face anything alone anymore. We're in this together now, forever."

And just like that — the tears came. Not out of sadness, but the kind that cleanse your soul and prepare it for something sacred.

Pranavi (tearing up):

"You always know just what to say, don't you? Thank you for being my anchor, Ayush. I love you."

Ayush (playfully):

"And I love you too. Now stop tearing up and finish getting ready, or I'll tell everyone you're late for your own wedding!"

She laughed again, through her tears, the kind of laugh that promises a thousand more just like it in the years to come.

Outside, the drums began to play softly. The sky turned a shade deeper. A gentle wind passed through the house — one that smelled like roses, haldi, and forever.

And somewhere between that last laugh and the footsteps approaching her room, Pranavi took one long breath… the kind you take when you're about to step into the rest of your life.

....The house buzzed again. The door opened. Laughter filled the hallway. Somewhere, the band began to warm up, and a slow breeze fluttered in through the half-open window — carrying with it the scent of roses... and forever.

Chapter 2

A Land Called Home

"Mur Axom, mur praan..." — My Assam, my soul.

Somewhere in the tender clasp of the eastern hills, beneath skies that changed colors like old lullabies, lies a land where time slows, and hearts beat in rhythm with the rain. This land — Assam — wasn't just geography for Pranavi. It was memory. It was melody. It was home.

Here, the mighty Brahmaputra didn't just flow — he sang. Like an old grandfather humming an ageless tune, his waters cradled secrets, tears, and stories passed down in whispers. The Barak, his gentler cousin, tiptoed through the valleys, washing over rice paddies and prayers with equal grace.

In this land of green and gold, every leaf had a story, and every breeze carried the scent of kopou phool and monsoon dreams. Birds didn't just fly — they recited morning hymns. Xorai stood proud in living rooms, holding offerings of love and legacy. Bihu, with its pepa and dhol, wasn't a festival — it was a feeling stitched into the heartbeats of its people.

Tucked within this fragrant soil was a little town called Duliajan — not grand, not loud, but brimming with soul. It was the kind of town where doors were left open, and lives were lived out loud — in the shared silence of dusk, in the chorus of frogs after rain, in the smell of mustard oil on winter mornings. Duliajan, was not just a dot on a map, but a world in itself — quiet yet alive, humble yet full of heart. Here, people weren't just neighbours; they were kin. Joys were shared like sweets, and sorrows divided like evening tea. Compassion flowed effortlessly.

In Duliajan stood a house like no other — not because of its walls, but because of the seven hearts that kept it warm. Six brothers and one sister — a constellation of love that never dimmed, no matter how cloudy the skies. Their love for one another was the kind that held storms at bay. The house echoed with laughter, teasing, and the kind of warmth only unity can bring.

When the eldest son of the family was blessed with a baby girl, the sun seemed to shine a little brighter that day. That little girl was **Pranavi** — the one who would bring light, softness, and quiet strength into everyone's life.

She was the hibiscus that bloomed even on rainy days. The laughter that echoed louder than the television. The little hand that tugged at her father's kurta, asking "Deuta, moi ki xundor?" — Papa, am I beautiful? And he would always answer, "You are the sunrise after the longest storm."

Pranavi grew up wrapped in love. Her world was a symphony of affection — doting parents, protective uncles, playful cousins, and her grandparents who carried stories in their wrinkles. Her mother, the wind beneath her wings, made sure she was nurtured in every way — enrolling her in painting, dancing, singing, and everything that could spark a new joy. Her father, gentle yet firm, was her first hero — the kind of man who believed that kindness was strength.

To the world, she was a bright child. To her family, she was everything.

Her grandmother, wise like the moon, would hum old lullabies as she braided her hair. Her grandfather would always say, "Girls should be like the ocean — calm and serene on the surface, but vast and powerful underneath." Pranavi never fully understood what he meant back then. But life — with all its storms and silences — eventually taught her.

She learned that calm wasn't weakness, it was control. Serenity wasn't surrender, it was strength.

And like the ocean, she carried worlds within her — unseen, unspoken, but mighty. Her uncles spoiled her with narikolor laru and paper boats. She has a younger brother, Nabarghya and her cousins - Pari, Kanak, and Satya. They used to build forts with her under mosquito nets, believing they were in another world. Always on the go. The home was like a huge fort where they always used to play hide and seek. Always on each others side. Her days were filled with games in the courtyard, mango-stained laughter, and hushed secrets exchanged under star-lit skies. Festivals were a riot of colors, food, and rituals. Her grandmother would braid hibiscus flowers into her hair during Bihu, whispering blessings in her ear. Her uncles, tired after long days, always had time for a story or a shared joke. Her cousins were her partners in chaos and dreams alike.

Her father, her anchor, showered her with gifts - not just for her but for all the children of the family.

Life in Duliajan wasn't perfect. But it was pure.

Each day was wrapped in the scent of home-cooked rice, the sound of the Naamghar bell, the crackle of radio dramas, and the ever-present hum of togetherness. Love was never spoken loudly — it was served on plates, packed in school tiffins, sewn into blouses by motherly hands, or hidden in letters written in Oxomiya.

There was something quietly magical about her childhood — the kind of magic that doesn't scream but stays with you forever.

Her parents were her world — her roots and her stem. Her father, the unshakable foundation beneath her dreams, and her mother, the ever-supportive trunk who held her upright through every storm. Together, they made her feel invincible. Pranavi grew up with an unwavering belief that no matter what came her way, they would always be her eternal protectors — the quiet guardians of her joy, the gentle keepers of her heart.

In her mind, she built a fairyland—a world crafted entirely by her imagination, where love was pure and perfect, and where no one entered without her permission. She dreamed of the day her soulmate would arrive, sweeping her off her feet in a poetic whirlwind of destiny.

Pranavi's story is one of joy and innocence, hope and dreams, woven into the lush fabric of Assam's beauty. Her journey was just beginning, but her heart carried a lifetime of stories waiting to unfold.

And now, on her wedding day, draped in silk and memories, Pranavi stood in Dehradun — far from Duliajan, but never without it.

She wore her hometown like a second skin. In the way her voice softened at the word "Maa." In the way she looked at hibiscus, jasmine (mogra/ bela phool) and parijat (night jasmine/ harsingar) flowers and smiled. In the quiet strength that told her she could start a new life, and still carry the old one in her soul.

Before stepping out, she whispered toward the open window, as if the wind would carry it home -

"Moi aahi asu. Bhal paai thakiba." — I'm leaving now. Stay loved."

Chapter 3

Whispers in the Shadows

"One rotten apple spoils the whole barrel," they say.

And for little Pranavi, that truth arrived early — bitter, uninvited, and close to home.

In a house once brimming with laughter and unshakable love, a quiet shadow began to stretch across her world. Her aunt — sharp-tongued and cold-eyed — wore envy like a second skin. It wasn't the kind that screamed. It whispered... in taunts, comparisons, and barbed silence.

Pranavi's academic brilliance, her innocent pride in report cards and school trophies, became a thorn to her aunt — a constant reminder of what her own children were not. Every certificate Pranavi brought home was met not with praise, but with thinly veiled mockery.

"Marks don't make a person great," she would mutter. "Let's see how far she really goes."

But Pranavi never answered back.

Her mother had taught her that silence was sometimes louder than words.

"Let your actions speak," she would say. "And when you speak, let it be with grace."

So, she smiled. She helped set the dinner table. She fetched water when elders asked. And in the quiet of her room, she wept sometimes — not because the words hurt, but because they shouldn't have.

The house, once full of joy, now echoed with tension. Arguments flared among the elders like monsoon tempests — sharp, sudden, and always about something. But no matter where the storm began, it always circled back to one name — her father's.

"The eldest should do more." "He's just a burden." "Everyone's carrying his weight."

These weren't whispered. They were thrown like knives.

And though she was just a child, Pranavi heard them all.

She would sit in corners — her legs tucked in, a half-read book in her lap — her mind drifting elsewhere.

Conscience: "Why do they keep saying such things about my father? He works so hard... don't they see it?"

Pranavi (to herself): "I know. He's always fixing things, bringing sweets, making sure we all have what we need. But... what if they're right? What if he's not doing enough for them?"

Conscience (firmly): "No, Pranavi. You've seen him. You've seen how he comes home late, how he wraps gifts not just for you, but for all the cousins. How he gives and never expects anything back. They only see the surface. You know the soul."

Pranavi (tearing up): "But why don't they understand? Why does it have to be this way? Why are they hurting him... and me?"

There were no answers. Only the birth of a quiet resolve.

From that day, she vowed to be his shadow of strength. Even if she could not defend him out loud, she would love him louder in silence.

This chapter in her childhood didn't end with a scream. It ended in whispers, in aching silence, in folded hands and tear-streaked cheeks. It marked the first time Pranavi realized that not all wounds bleed — some just bruise the heart quietly.

And even as the pages of life turned, this one... never really closed.

Chapter 4

When the Sky Fell Silent

There are moments in life that arrive without warning —

that tear through your world without knocking.

For Pranavi, that moment came like a storm…

swift, cruel, and utterly unforgiving.

This storm didn't just wreak havoc on the surroundings - it tore apart the very roots of Pranavi's family. It shook the foundation of the tree that had always stood tall and unshaken. The "roots" - her father, began to wither, and the "stem" - her mother, bore the brunt of holding things together, though cracks were beginning to show.

The Last Ordinary Evening

Just before the storm arrived, there was one evening — soft, ordinary, and now etched in gold.

Pranavi was sitting cross-legged on the floor, a plate of rice and aloo pitika in her lap, savoring every bite with the slow delight only a child can afford. Her father sat beside her, resting back on his palms, watching her eat with a quiet smile.

The television played something faint in the background — but the real warmth came from the moment between them.

He reached out, his fingers gently ruffling her hair.

"Are you doing alright, my little girl?" he asked, his voice a blend of mischief and melody.

She nodded shyly, her mouth too full to speak. Her eyes sparkled with the comfort of that touch — the kind of love that doesn't need to be earned, only felt.

Her father laughed softly and turned to her mother in the kitchen.

"You know, one day, when she grows up, she'll probably end up in your college. Can you imagine that? Mother and daughter, sharing the same campus?"

Her mother rolled her eyes with playful exasperation, but even she couldn't hide the smile that curved her lips.

Pranavi giggled, already imagining herself in a sari like her mother, walking the same corridors, making her parents proud.

That evening — simple, sweet, forgotten by the world — stayed with her long after everything else faded.

It became her last untouched memory.

The one she would hold onto tightly,

when all the others began to unravel.

At first, the health conditions of her father were small things - fatigue, paleness, a cough that lingered. But within weeks, those whispers of illness became sirens. He grew weaker, quieter… and suddenly, he was in the hospital.

The doctors' words were blunt, clinical — *liver cirrhosis, dangerously high blood pressure*. Pranavi was only eleven. She didn't understand the medical terms, but she understood the looks — the worry etched on her mother's face, the hushed whispers in the corridors, the prayers said with trembling hands.

He was vomiting blood. His body — once strong, capable, and full of life — now lay beneath white sheets, fighting battles it could not win.

At home, Pranavi took on responsibilities too big for her age.

Every day, when her mother returned from the hospital to quickly gather fresh clothes for her husband, Pranavi would be waiting. She would take the stained shirts from her mother's trembling hands — shirts blotched with blood, stiff with fear — and without flinching, she would begin to wash them.

With her small hands, she scrubbed and scrubbed, even when the stains refused to fade.

Pranavi (to herself, while washing):

"Deuta won't like seeing his clothes dirty. He always says a person should look neat and tidy, even when they're sick." (Her father used to wear gracefully and he was fond of clothes which would make him more handsome).

Conscience (softly):

"But will he even wear them again? What if—"

Pranavi (interrupting):

"No. Don't say that. He will come back. He has to. I'll keep these ready for him. He'll be proud of me."

She folded them carefully, stacking them in a corner of her cupboard — as if order could protect her from the chaos outside.

And then she would wait.

She waited by the gate every evening, hoping, wishing, praying. Every sound — a creaking hinge, a pair of footsteps — made her heart leap.

Pranavi (whispering to the gate):

"Papa, please come home. I've been good. I've done everything you'd want me to. Just come back… please."

Her conscience, quieter now, watched her with a sad stillness.

But the gate never opened.

And then… the news came.

There was no dramatic cry, no loud breakdown.

Only a silence so heavy it could crush the heart.

Her father was gone.

Every day, she checked the gate, her hope unwavering, her little heart yearning for a miracle. The neat stack of washed clothes remained untouched, a silent witness to her belief. But no miracle came. The gate stayed closed.

At the funeral, surrounded by white flowers and the chant of sacred verses, Pranavi refused to believe it. She clung to the fantasy that it was a mistake — that maybe the body wasn't his. That he would return… any day now… with his old smile and warm eyes.

The folded shirts in her cupboard remained untouched. They became relics of hope. She would look at them every night, tracing the fabric with her fingers.

She never said goodbye.

In the days that followed, grief seeped into every corner of their lives — shapeless, formless, but overwhelmingly present. It came dressed in silence, in questions that had no answers, and in the hollow spaces where once there had been laughter and love. The world outside continued to move, but for Pranavi, time had collapsed into a slow, aching blur.

She didn't shed a single tear.

Not because she didn't want to. But because she couldn't. It was as if her body had frozen in time, her mind refusing to believe the truth her eyes had witnessed. Her father — the man who had once lifted her onto his shoulders and made the world look small — was gone.

Her temperature soared, her body giving up in protest to the pain that had no outlet. She lay in bed, feverish and pale, watching the ceiling blur into nothingness. She didn't speak. Didn't ask. Didn't resist. The heartbreak had drained her of every drop of strength. She was hollow — a shell of the girl she had been. Her father — her pillar, her hero — was gone.

And amidst the chaos of rituals and whispers and condolences, in the verandah outside her home, her younger brother, barely old enough to tie his own shoelaces not long ago, was now entrusted with the last rites. He was only a boy, five years younger than her — soft-hearted, sensitive — and yet, that day, he was the man of the house. He tried to make sense of the unfamiliar silence. He was just five years younger than her, still holding on to the innocence of boyhood.

As they prepared their father's body for the ceremonial bath in the stillness of early morning, when the moon still clung to the sky and the air was sharp with dew, he looked around, wide-eyed, confused.

"But… won't Deuta feel cold?" he asked softly while watching as water was poured over his father's body. "Why are we bathing him so early in the morning?"

The words fell into the air like broken glass — fragile, piercing. And yet, no one could answer. No words would've made sense in that moment, not to a child trying to reconcile love with loss. The priests looked away. The elders swallowed hard. Grief caught in everyone's throats, but the boy's question, innocent and aching, hung in the air like sacred truth — innocent, piercing, unforgettable

And in that moment, even the skies seemed to grieve.

Pranavi's father was the kind of man whose presence could quiet an entire room — not out of fear, but out of reverence. Tall and dignified, with eyes that held both wisdom and compassion, he carried the silence of strength and the calm of a man who had seen life in all its shades.

In their town, people spoke of him with both respect and caution — not because he demanded it, but because he deserved it. His principles were never shouted; they were lived, quietly and consistently. He believed in doing good, not for recognition, but because kindness was stitched into his soul. If someone was in need, he would be the first to offer help, often without letting anyone know. That quiet nobility — Pranavi carried it in her blood.

To his family, he was a gentle giant. He found joy in the simplest things — a shared meal, laughter echoing in the veranda, an evening spent telling stories to his children. He wanted nothing more than to live a life surrounded by love, by togetherness, by the music of everyday happiness.

And then, there was his smile.

Oh, that smile — so effortless, so pure. It lit up his entire face, revealing teeth so perfect they looked as though they had been carved by an artist. His smile wasn't just beautiful — it was reassuring, like a soft promise that no matter how hard the world became, kindness would still exist.

When he smiled, it was as if the world paused for a moment — not because it was grand, but because it was genuine. And when he spoke, his words stayed with you, like a soft echo in the heart.

Pranavi often said that if the universe ever gave form to kindness, strength, and grace, it would look exactly like her father.

Even today, when she closes her eyes, she can feel his hand on her head, steady and warm — as if silently reminding her, "No matter where you are, I'm always with you."

Her mother, now both parent and protector, stood strong... at least on the outside. But Pranavi saw it — the cracks. The silent cries behind closed doors. The way her mother's hands shook while tying her braid in the morning.

Their family, once a fortress of togetherness, grew colder. Her brother, Nabarghya, was sent away to a boarding school in Shillong, Meghalaya. Friends were no longer welcome in the house. Birthdays passed quietly, unsung. Each year, her mother would quietly take her to the nearby temple, offering prayers instead of cake. Pranavi stood still, palms folded, eyes closed — a child wishing for joy in a place where grief had built its home.

She never asked for more. She knew there was none to give.

The child in her learned early — some losses don't just take people, they take colors too.

Even the family cars, once a shared joy, were suddenly out of reach.

It was as if losing her father meant losing everything — her voice, her space, her right to joy.

And then came the final blow.

The final blow to her dignity came one fateful day. One afternoon, out of pure kindness, Pranavi gave two of her classmates a lift home. Her aunt saw it… and slapped her in public.

No questions. No conversation. Just a blow that shattered more than skin.

Conscience (angrily):

"Why do you let them treat you like this? Stand up for yourself!"

Pranavi (resolutely):

"No. I won't fight back. I'll prove them wrong… not with words, but with who I become."

The summer that stole her father had also taken away her voice.

Pranavi didn't inform her teachers, or the school management. Not out of rebellion or secrecy — but out of fear. A child's fear. That irrational yet all-consuming dread that if people knew about her grief, they would look at her differently.

The summer vacation was unusually long that year — three whole months. Plenty of time for the world to change behind closed doors, while school buildings remained still and silent.

When the gates finally reopened and students returned, carrying stories of family trips and mango-laced afternoons, Pranavi carried something else — silence. And a weight no child should ever bear.

She tried to blend in, to be the same old Pranavi — smiling at jokes, nodding along, pretending that her world hadn't collapsed.

But children, even at their most innocent, can sometimes be unkind.

One girl — someone she had once called a friend — found out. How, Pranavi never knew. Maybe overheard whispers, maybe a relative talking too loudly, maybe just the way grief clung to her eyes like dried salt.

One afternoon, between the shaded corridors and whispered homework answers, the girl cornered her.

"I know what happened," she hissed. "And if you don't help me in class, I'll tell everyone. I'll tell the whole school about your father."

The words hit her like a slap. Cold. Cruel. Calculated.

Pranavi stood frozen, her lips trembling, eyes wide with panic. "Please," she whispered, "please don't."

She wasn't afraid of sympathy — she was afraid of isolation. Of being outcasted from her friend groups, of whispers following her in the hallways. In her young mind, grief was a stamp — one that made her different. One that people would never let her forget.

But the truth was far kinder than her fear. Her classmates, if they had known, wouldn't have turned away. But Pranavi didn't know that then. All she knew was fear — of losing more than she already had.

So she stayed quiet.

Did the homework. Shared notes. Smiled when she didn't feel like it.

Because sometimes, even children learn how to wear masks long before they understand why they're needed.

Growing up, Pranavi learned far too early that not all dangers look like monsters. Some sit across the table, with books and pens, disguised as mentors.

She had begun taking tuitions from a reputed math teacher in the neighborhood — a man known for his sharp mind and structured lessons. But week after week, during those quiet study hours, his hands would wander beneath the table, brushing against her knees. A casual pat here, a gentle nudge there — always masked by smiles and equations.

She didn't have the vocabulary to name it, but she knew something wasn't right.

At another point, a music teacher — the kind who praised her voice and asked her to sing louder — would find reasons to stand behind her, placing a hand too low on her back, lingering just a second too long. Again, she stayed quiet. Confused. Unsettled. Afraid.

Back then, these things weren't talked about openly. Words like assault or harassment were not part of the everyday language in her world. What was she supposed to say? And to whom?

But one day, after summoning all the strength she could gather from her growing storm of discomfort, she told her mother. She didn't explain everything — she didn't know how — but the tremble in her voice said enough.

Her mother, to her credit, acted without delay. She stopped the tuitions immediately and started teaching Pranavi herself, determined to protect her daughter's safety even if it meant adding to her own burdens.

But the pain didn't end there.

At home, other wounds formed — quieter, but equally sharp. Her uncle and aunt, instead of being pillars of support, became sources of constant humiliation. They'd comment with cruel indifference:

"You're looking older than your age now."

"Have you noticed how fat you're getting lately?"

Their words were laced with judgment and shame, thrown casually into dinner conversations like spices, leaving Pranavi to swallow bitterness she hadn't asked for.

And when it wasn't about her, it was about her mother.

A single mother raising two children — a woman who dared to be strong — was easy fodder for gossip. They mocked her strength, masked their scorn in smiles, and whispered judgments as though they were facts.

Pranavi internalized it all. The inappropriate touches. The body-shaming. The insults against the woman she loved most.

She didn't know where one wound ended and another began.

But slowly, silently, she made herself a promise:

This cycle will end with me.

And that promise — though whispered in fear and made from pain — would become her guiding light in the years to come.

She turned her pain into purpose.

She threw herself into her books, competitions, school performances — anything that could lift her above the noise. She began to rebuild herself, quietly but fiercely.

She had learned too early that life isn't fair.

But she also learned that strength sometimes grows not in defiance… but in quiet dignity.

And in her heart, she kept one memory locked like treasure —

a final meal, a final moment, her father's hand gently stroking her head.

"Are you doing alright, my little girl?" he had asked, eyes full of love.

She hadn't answered then. But now, years later, through every test, every tear, every step forward…

She whispered back:

"Yes, Deuta… I'm trying."

Chapter 5

The Girl Who Built Walls

As the years passed, the little girl who once waited at the gate with hope in her eyes...

grew into a young woman who carried her grief like an invisible crown.

Pranavi was no longer the fragile child in the corner.

She was fierce in her silence, graceful in her discipline, and rooted in values that became the unshakable spine of her existence.

But these values... they came with a cost.

They were rules she carved into herself —

not taught, but born from pain.

Rules that kept her from breaking,

and also kept her from blooming.

She didn't cry easily.

She didn't speak much of herself.

Even in front of her mother — her anchor, her only constant — she wore a quiet armor.

She smiled often, but her joy was measured.

She succeeded often, but her pride was humble.

She lived life like a handwritten schedule — neat, contained, underlined with perfection.

And her mother?

She saw it all — the strength, the ache, the restraint.

She didn't interfere. She only stayed close.

A silent cheerleader in every auditorium, every report card meeting, every moment when the world clapped but didn't know the cost behind the applause.

When the time came, Pranavi left home to chase higher studies — earning a spot in one of India's most reputed colleges. A campus filled with promise, competition, and color.

Here, a new chapter quietly unfurled.

Among fresh notebooks and unfamiliar faces, she met Shaila — wild-hearted, loud, full of laughter. Everything Pranavi was not.

Shaila wore her emotions on her sleeve. She cried in class, danced in corridors, laughed too loud in the canteen. She was sunshine in sneakers.

And somehow… they clicked.

Shaila brought chaos. Pranavi brought calm.

Together, they balanced each other.

Shaila taught her that it was okay to lose control sometimes.

And Pranavi reminded her to pause and breathe.

On the other hand, there was Shravani — a rare mirror to Pranavi's soul. Hailing from the same land of Assam, Shravani carried the same warmth in her smile and that familiar rhythm in her words. Their connection wasn't forged through time, but through a quiet understanding that bloomed almost instantly. Together, they shared not just laughter over mundane misadventures, but a sense of home that was hard to find in a world constantly shifting. Whether it was over chai on rainy evenings or through shared silences, Shravani became that comforting presence who reminded Pranavi of who she was before the world asked her to be stronger.

Over time, Pranavi's name echoed through campus — not just as a brilliant student, but as someone people trusted. Her classmates confided in her. Professors praised her. Juniors admired her.

She had become a lighthouse.

But even lighthouses are lonely.

While others cried and laughed openly, Pranavi kept her oceans locked within.

She had learned not to trust feelings — not others', not even her own.

She was the girl people leaned on.

But when night came and the hostel lights dimmed, she often lay awake…

wishing someone would lean on her,

without her having to ask.

She doubted deeply, feared silently, and protected her heart with every ounce of logic she could gather.

Her confidence was real.

Her achievements, undeniable.

But behind all of it… was a quiet yearning.

A longing to belong — to someone, somewhere, someday.

She had built walls so strong, not even love could find its way in.

And yet, in a time of absolute despair, something broke through…

And just as she was beginning to breathe in the rhythm of college life, life pulled her into a storm she never saw coming.

Her cousin **Pari** — only a year younger than her, more sister than cousin — had been diagnosed with **polyp-like growths** in her intestines. Cancerous, the doctors said. Aggressive. Unforgiving.

The word itself hit like a cold slap.

Cancer.

It wasn't supposed to happen to people her age.

Not Pari — the girl who once danced with her during Bihu, who shared beds, secrets, and stolen mangoes in the summer.

Pari was admitted to a private hospital in Delhi — just a few kilometers from Pranavi's campus, but the emotional distance felt like a galaxy.

The family was in panic. Her parents looked like shadows of themselves. The doctors had tried everything — and then one night, they said something that chilled Pranavi to her bones:

"We can't find her pulse."

She rushed to the ICU, the fluorescent lights too bright, the air too still. She wasn't ready to say goodbye. Not like this. Not now.

She walked in slowly, her palms clammy, her heart a knot.

Pari lay motionless, her body pale, her chest barely rising. Pranavi reached for her hand — trembling, cold, yet still hers. She held it tightly, her own tears falling onto their clasped fingers.

"Pari... you don't get to leave me like this," she whispered, her voice cracking,

"We still have too much to do. You promised we'd grow old together... remember?"

And then—

something shifted.

A beep. A murmur. A movement.

The doctors rushed in.

A nurse gasped.

A voice called out, stunned — "We're getting a pulse."

The very moment Pranavi gripped Pari's hand,

life came back —

fragile, flickering… but real.

It wasn't science.

It wasn't logic.

It was love.

The days that followed were slow but sure. Pari's condition began to improve. The hopelessness in the doctors' eyes slowly faded, replaced by cautious optimism. Eventually, she healed. Slowly, but fully.

And she lived.

She went on to chase her own dreams.

But for Pranavi, that moment remained etched forever — the moment she sat by the ICU bed, thinking she'd lost her sister… only to feel her hand come back to life in hers.

She had been holding herself together for years.

But that night — for someone else — she held on with every ounce of belief she had left.

Not because she had hope…

but because she became hope.

That's who she was —

The girl who held on,

even when she was falling apart inside.

Chapter 6

When Love Felt Like a Dream

During her graduation days, Pranavi's life took an unexpected turn when she met Karan. He was everything a girl might admire — handsome, smart, and charming. One day, to her surprise, Karan approached her with a warm smile and a simple proposal: to be friends. It was a gesture that caught her off guard, but also one that planted a seed of curiosity in her heart.

Karan wasn't particularly focused on his studies, but when it came to Pranavi, he was attentive and thoughtful. He respected her deeply, going out of his way to make sure he never annoyed or upset her. His small acts of kindness, his easy laughter, and the way he made her feel seen — it all slowly worked its way into her heart.

Before long, Pranavi found herself looking forward to seeing him every day. The thought of Karan arriving at college filled her with a happiness she couldn't quite explain. Her world seemed brighter, her steps lighter, as though nothing else mattered as much. Deep down, she had a feeling that Karan liked her too.

At the hostel, her friends became her confidants. Night after night, she would chatter about Karan, her eyes lighting up at every mention of his name. Her friends teased her endlessly, but it only added to the magic of those days. For Pranavi, the love she felt was pure and consuming. Every second, every minute, her thoughts revolved around him. It was as though her heart had found its anchor in his presence.

But as graduation approached, reality began to intrude on her fairytale. The last days of college came and went, and Pranavi started to realize that what she cherished so deeply might have been just a fleeting dream. The world she had built in her heart started to crumble, piece by piece. Her intuition, her hopes, her feelings — all of it felt like an illusion.

Her heart broke into countless pieces. The once-vibrant Pranavi was now drowning in despair. Her closest friends tried to console her, urging her to move on, reminding her that this wasn't the end. But their words barely reached her. The pain was too raw, the void too deep.

To make matters worse, Karan — once her source of light — turned cold. One day, towards the very end of their college days, he shouted at her over the phone.

"I live with my family, so don't try and call me ever again," he barked, before abruptly hanging up.

His words hit her like a slap. Not just in tone, but in what they represented — complete dismissal, complete erasure. It was the final blow to an already bleeding heart.

Depression set in like an unwelcome guest. Pranavi couldn't eat, drink, or sleep. Her mind was in turmoil, and her body bore the consequences. She moved through her days in a haze, narrowly escaping accidents caused by her distracted state. In her darkest moments, she even thought of harming herself, the weight of her emotions too much to bear.

One sunny day, her phone rang. It was her mother.

(Pranavi hesitates before answering, her voice shaky. The sound of her familiar voice opens a floodgate of emotions.)

Mother: "Pranavi? What's wrong? Are you crying? What happened?"

Pranavi (trying to compose herself): "Nothing, Maa... I'm just... tired."

Mother (firmly): "Don't lie to me. I can hear it in your voice. Tell me what's bothering you."

Pranavi wanted to spill everything — the heartbreak, the pain — but she couldn't. She knew her mother would be furious if she found out. Instead, she broke down, her sobs escaping uncontrollably.

Pranavi (barely able to speak): "Maa, I don't know how to explain it... I just feel so lost. Everything feels so heavy, and I don't know what to do."

Her mother's voice softened, but there was a firmness beneath her concern.

Mother: "Beta, take a deep breath and talk to me. Whatever it is, we'll figure it out. Are you feeling unwell? Is something happening at college?"

Pranavi (trembling): "I don't know, Maa. I feel like... like I'm failing at everything. Nothing makes sense anymore. I just want to come home."

Mother: "You're not failing, Pranavi. You're just going through a rough patch. It happens to everyone, beta. But you can't let it take over. You're stronger than this."

Pranavi (tearfully): "I don't feel strong, Maa. I feel... broken. I can't eat, I can't sleep. My mind won't stop running in circles, and I don't know how to make it stop."

Mother (now deeply worried): "Pranavi, listen to me. You are not broken. You're just overwhelmed. It's okay to feel like this sometimes, but you can't give up. Come home for a few days. Let me take care of you."

Pranavi (softly): "No, Maa. I don't want to trouble you. You've already done so much for me."

Mother (with a stern yet loving tone): "Enough of this nonsense. You are my daughter. Nothing matters to me more than you. You are never a burden, do you understand? You've always been my brave girl, and I won't let you face this alone."

Pranavi (sniffling): "Maa, I'm trying... but it's so hard."

Mother: "I know it's hard, beta. But you've faced tough times before, and you've come out stronger every time. Focus on what's important — your studies, your dreams. These feelings won't last forever, I promise. Just take it one day at a time."

Her mother's words were the lifeline Pranavi needed. Slowly, she began to rebuild herself, step by painful step.

Yet, in the quiet corners of her heart, a tiny glimmer of hope remained — a fragile belief that Karan might still return someday. It wasn't a hope she spoke of, but it lingered, like the last ember of a fire she wasn't ready to let go of entirely.

Pranavi's journey through heartbreak and healing wasn't just a chapter in her life — it was a battle, a transformation, and a testament to her resilience.

Chapter 7

The First Taste of Flight

Hope is a strange thing. It lifts you up, gives you strength, and yet, often leaves you with nothing but longing. For Pranavi, hope was a thread that held her life together — fragile yet unbroken. Life begins with hope and, somehow, ends with it too.

With her graduation complete, it was time for Pranavi to take the next big step. Determined to achieve greater heights, she threw herself into preparing for management entrance exams. After months of effort, she secured admission to a reputed B-School and began her post-graduation journey.

Pranavi thrived in this new phase of her life. As always, she stood out — not just for her academic performance but for her kindness and soft-spoken nature. She believed deeply in treating everyone with respect, ensuring her words never hurt anyone. This gentle demeanor, coupled with her willingness to help others, made her beloved by both her peers and professors.

It wasn't long before she formed a close-knit group of friends. Aarushi, Aaditya, Vivaan, Rohit, Charu, and Yamini became her constants. Together, they brought life to the classroom — passing comments, sharing laughs, and working on group projects. Their bond made even mundane activities like PowerPoint presentations and scoldings from teachers feel like cherished memories in the making.

Aaditya, Vivaan and Rohit, bound by their "Bong Connection," were inseparable, while Pranavi and Charu shared a cozy PG in Gurgaon. Aarushi and Yamini also lived in Gurgaon, though in different locations, and their meetups were mostly limited to college or nearby eateries. Yet, whether it was assignments, exams, or just life, their group had a sacred tradition of gathering at the boys' house to study — or, more often, to laugh the night away.

Pranavi found herself immersed in the camaraderie, even as her friends introduced her to little "tactics" like proxy attendance, which she initially hesitated to join but soon found amusing. It was a time of carefree freedom, the kind she had never experienced before. Away from the structured boundaries of home, she tasted independence for the first time, savoring the sweetness of unbridled laughter and self-discovery.

Her professors noticed her dedication and unique spirit. One day, during a Retail domain lecture, a professor paused mid-sentence and said, "Mark my words, Pranavi. One day, you'll do something big. Who knows — you might even become the next Indra Nooyi!"

The compliment left her momentarily speechless. To be compared to someone as remarkable as Indra Nooyi was both humbling and inspiring. It planted a seed of ambition within her — a belief that she was meant for something extraordinary.

In those vibrant, bustling days of post-graduation, Pranavi wasn't just finding direction; she was beginning to carve her own path. She was stepping into her own, armed with hope, resilience, and a newfound sense of freedom.

Life, for the first time, felt like it was hers to shape.

In the warm haze of those college corridors, Pranavi felt herself slowly softening.

Not breaking — just becoming.

The ache from her past still lived in quiet corners of her heart, but it no longer ruled her. It had taught her things no textbook ever could — about strength, about letting go, and about rebuilding… brick by brick, breath by breath.

And in this season of light, her friends became her refuge. They laughed together, stayed up till 3 AM perfecting marketing case studies (and sometimes just ordering momos), cribbed about grades, and whispered secrets during boring lectures. There was a rhythm now — something almost sacred in their chaos.

Among them, one person began to stand out — though neither of them said it out loud.

Aaditya.

He was unlike anyone she had known — quietly confident, often teasing, and maddeningly easy-going. He didn't push his way into her life, but somehow, he was always there — offering his opinion with a smirk, stealing her fries, or walking her to the metro without being asked.

Their bond began in shared group chats and project banter, but something deeper brewed underneath. Pranavi, who had mastered the art of restraint, found herself looking forward to his messages. His presence was calming — like the smell of earth after rain.

There was one evening, after a hectic presentation, when they were walking home side by side.

"You know you're a perfectionist, right?" Aaditya teased, nudging her shoulder.

"Someone has to balance out your 'wing-it-and-pray' strategy," she retorted, eyes twinkling.

He laughed, that low, rumbling sound that always made her stomach flip.

"Well, your perfectionism worked. We nailed that pitch," he said, holding the door open for her. **"Even the professor smiled. That's historic."**

And it was in such moments — the small ones, the in-between silences — that something invisible wove itself between them.

Soon after, the announcement came — **the Annual Cultural Fest**.

The entire campus lit up. Banners were unfurled, music filled the air, and every classroom buzzed with excitement.

At first, Pranavi was thrilled by the idea. She envisioned hours of practice, perfect harmonies, and a performance that would leave the audience spellbound. But reality turned out to be far less cooperative, thanks to Aaditya's laid-back attitude.

One afternoon during practice, she stormed into the room to find Aaditya sprawled on a chair, munching on chips and humming absentmindedly.

Pranavi (exasperated): "Aaditya! Are you even taking this seriously? We need to rehearse, and you're sitting here like it's a holiday picnic!"

Aaditya (grinning): "Relax, Pranavi. Why are you so worked up? We've got this covered."

Pranavi (fuming): "Got this covered? You've barely practiced. You're going to stand on stage and wing it? That's your plan?"

Aaditya (laughing): "Exactly! Trust me, my natural charm will win them over. They won't even notice if I miss a note."

Pranavi threw her hands up in frustration, muttering under her breath, "Impossible! You're absolutely impossible."

Despite his teasing, Aaditya finally relented and joined her for practice. But true to his personality, he found every opportunity to crack jokes and pull her leg, leaving Pranavi torn between irritation and laughter.

Aaditya (mocking her seriousness): "You know, if they gave awards for most intense rehearsals, you'd win hands down."

Pranavi (glaring): "And if they gave awards for being the biggest distraction, guess who'd take that trophy?"

After days of chaotic rehearsals filled with arguments, laughter, and a few last-minute adjustments, the much-awaited fest day finally arrived. The campus was alive with vibrant decorations, cheering crowds, and an electric atmosphere.

When it was their turn to perform, Pranavi took a deep breath, silently praying that Aaditya wouldn't mess it up. As the music started, the banter disappeared, and they locked into their duet. Their voices blended harmoniously, creating a performance that was far better than Pranavi had dared to hope. Aaditya, true to his word, carried himself with a charming ease that delighted the audience, while Pranavi's dedication and vocal precision shone through every note.

As the final notes faded, the crowd erupted into cheers and applause. Friends and classmates hooted, clapped, and cheered for their effort.

Aaditya (with a triumphant wink): "See? Told you we'd pull it off."

Pranavi (shaking her head, laughing): "I can't believe I doubted you. But don't let it go to your head — you were still a pain."

Aaditya (grinning): "Admit it, Pranavi. You had fun. Even with me around."

Even though they didn't win first place, the appreciation they received from the crowd was more than enough for Pranavi. It was a moment to cherish — proof that sometimes, even amidst chaos and irritation, unexpected joys can bloom.

Chapter 8

The Beginning of Something Else

Over time, Pranavi and Aaditya became inseparable, their bond growing stronger with each passing day. They spent hours chatting about everything under the sun, their conversations flowing effortlessly. Arguments over trivial matters became a daily ritual — playful fights that often ended in laughter.

Whenever Pranavi faced a problem, Aaditya was the first person she called. His words had a way of calming her, making the world feel less overwhelming. No matter how complicated the issue, it seemed to untangle itself after a talk with him. It wasn't long before Pranavi found herself seeking his opinion on almost every decision she made. Apart from her mother, Aaditya was the only person she trusted completely — someone she could rely on with her eyes closed.

There was something about him that made her feel at ease, like she could share anything without fear of judgment. He became her anchor, her go-to person, the one who made her feel safe. But as their bond deepened, so did a new, unfamiliar feeling stirring within her.

One evening, after a long conversation with Aaditya, Pranavi found herself sitting alone in her room, her thoughts swirling.

Inner Thought: "Why does everything feel so different when I'm talking to him? Why do I wait for his calls like this? Is this what they call..."

She shook her head, trying to dismiss the thought.

Pranavi (to herself): "No, no. This is just friendship. He's my best friend, nothing more."

But even as she tried to reason with herself, her heart whispered otherwise.

Inner Thought (persisting): "But why does your heart race every time he smiles at you? Why do you feel like everything will be okay as long as he's around?"

Pranavi (frustrated, softly): "Stop it. He doesn't see me that way. What if I ruin everything by even thinking like this?"

Her thoughts didn't relent.

Inner Thought: "But what if he does? What if you're not the only one feeling this way? What's stopping you from finding out?"

Pranavi sighed, hugging a pillow tightly, her mind a battlefield of emotions.

Pranavi (whispering): "I don't know. I'm scared. What if I lose him, even as a friend? I can't risk that."

Her feelings for Aaditya were no longer just those of friendship, but she was too confused — and too scared — to admit it to herself fully. For now, she decided to bury her thoughts, hoping the answers would reveal themselves with time.

Chapter 9

Of Dreams, Distances, and Dilemmas

The college was abuzz with excitement once again as preparations began for another grand event—this time, a campus-specific celebration. The event became a labor of love for the students, with everyone pouring their hearts and minds into their assigned tasks, no matter how small. It was a collective effort, driven by the shared goal of creating something extraordinary.

Pranavi, as always, was at the center of the action. She joined the Event Management team, eager to contribute to the planning and execution. To her surprise and delight, Aaditya, her singing partner and close friend, was also part of the same group. The duo quickly found themselves immersed in the whirlwind of responsibilities, juggling planning meetings, decorations, and endless brainstorming sessions.

Amidst the hustle and bustle, one of their professors approached them with a special request. "Pranavi, Aaditya," the professor said, "why don't the two of you prepare a couple of duet songs for the event? Your performance at the fest was a hit, and I'm sure the audience will love to see you two perform again."

They nodded in agreement, though the task added another layer of responsibility to their already packed schedules. But later that evening, Aaditya pulled Pranavi aside with an apologetic look.

"Aaditya, what's wrong?" she asked, sensing his unease.

"Pranavi, I'm really sorry," he said, hesitating slightly. "I won't be able to perform. My throat's been acting up, and the doctor said I need to rest it for a while."

Pranavi felt a wave of mixed emotions. Annoyance at his sudden withdrawal, worry about his health, and, underneath it all, disappointment.

"You could've told me earlier," she said, folding her arms. "But are you okay? Is it serious?"

"I'll be fine," Aaditya reassured her. "But there's something I need to ask."

A few days later, while riding together on his bike after an event meeting, Aaditya broke the silence.

"Pranavi, I want you to perform on that stage," he said, his voice steady despite the hum of the engine. "Please, do it for my sake. I know you can pull it off, even without me. You've got this incredible talent, and everyone should see it. Don't hold back just because I can't be there with you."

His words caught her off guard.

"You really think I can do this?" she asked softly.

"I don't just think," Aaditya said, glancing at her briefly with a small smile. "I know you can. You'll succeed, Pranavi. I have full faith in you."

"Okay," she said, a smile tugging at her lips. "But you'd better be there cheering the loudest in the crowd."

"Deal," he replied, grinning.

In their own ways, they always looked out for each other. Aaditya rarely expressed his feelings openly. But moments like these revealed the depth of his care, leaving Pranavi wondering just how much she truly meant to him.

Interlude: Pages from a Diary Never Sent

Sometimes, silence says more than words ever could...

✎ Pranavi's Diary, a page smeared with soft tears and soft hope

Somewhere in her small rented room in Pune, a warm yellow lamp flickers beside her bed. The city hums outside, but inside — Pranavi is quiet. She picks up her diary, its edges frayed and familiar, and begins to write...

Dear Diary,

They say when you miss someone deeply, it's not just the person you long for —

It's the version of yourself you were when they were around.

And maybe that's true.

Because every time I think of him, I remember not just his voice,

but the calm it brought to my chaos.

Not just his words, but how they made me believe in mine.

I don't know when the lines between friendship and love began to blur —

Maybe it was in a shared glance over chai,

or in the comfort of midnight calls when sleep refused
to come.

There's a strange beauty in unspoken things —

in feelings you carry in silence,

because the risk of losing what *is*

feels far greater than the hope of what *could be*.

But sometimes I wonder…

If I shouted all this into the wind,

Would the breeze carry it to him?

Would he smile? Would he pause?

Or would it vanish like a song played only once?

For now, I hold onto the little things —

His voice in my mind

when I'm doubting myself.

His laughter echoing on days I feel too small.

The thought of his faith in me

when mine begins to crumble.

And maybe that's enough for now.

Love,

Pranavi

Chapter 10

Beyond the Fest – Echoes of the Heart

As part of their curriculum, the time came for summer internships, and Pranavi found herself less than thrilled about her placement. She was assigned to a software company in Bangalore—a field she had no interest in. Frustrated, she shared her feelings with Aaditya during one of their late-night calls.

"Bangalore, Aaditya," she groaned. "And a software company of all places! This isn't what I wanted at all. I don't even know what I'll do there."

"Pranavi, calm down," Aaditya replied, his voice steady and reassuring. "It's not about the company; it's about the learning. Small or big, every place teaches you something. Trust me, you'll find value in this experience."

Reluctantly, she decided to give it a shot, and Aaditya's words soon proved true. Despite her initial reluctance, she discovered a supportive and down-to-earth work environment. The team welcomed her like one of their own, and within two months, she received an appreciation letter from the company's CEO—a moment that left her both proud and humbled.

Every Friday, she organized co-curricular activities for the employees, infusing a sense of camaraderie into the workplace. Although she was enjoying her time there, she couldn't help but miss her friends, especially Aaditya.

Meanwhile, Aaditya was in Pune, interning with a well-known brand in the research domain. Despite the physical distance, they stayed connected, their late-night conversations becoming the highlight of Pranavi's days.

"Aaditya," she confessed one evening, "everything feels better after talking to you. It's like... like the world isn't so overwhelming anymore."

"That's because you overthink, Pranavi," he teased lightly. "And I'm here to stop you from driving yourself crazy."

Her mornings began with a call to wake him up, and her nights ended with their long chats. Aaditya had become her anchor, the one person she could trust blindly apart from her mother. For Pranavi, it felt as though her entire world revolved around him.

During her time in Bangalore, she discovered that Rohit, one of her close friends, was also interning in the same city. They met occasionally, catching up on life and reminiscing about their college days. However, over time, Rohit's feelings for her grew stronger.

One day, over coffee, he hesitantly confessed, "Pranavi, I've been meaning to tell you... I think I'm in love with you."

Startled, Pranavi froze for a moment before carefully replying, "Rohit, you're a good friend to me, but I don't feel the same way. I'm really sorry if this hurts you, but I can't lead you on."

Rohit nodded, masking his disappointment. Pranavi tried to maintain their friendship, but she kept a healthy distance to avoid any misunderstandings.

Later that evening, she called Aaditya to share what had happened.

"Why does this keep happening?" she sighed. "I don't want to hurt anyone, Aaditya, but I can't control how they feel."

"It's not your fault, Pranavi," he reassured her. "You've always been honest, and that's all you can do. Just be yourself, and everything will fall into place."

Their bond grew stronger with every call. Whenever Pranavi felt lonely or overwhelmed, Aaditya was her refuge. Even when misunderstandings arose, driven by others who tried to influence her negatively, Aaditya's calm and wise nature kept their friendship intact.

"Aaditya," she said during one of their calls, "I don't know what I'd do without you. You're the only one who truly understands me."

"And I always will," he replied, his voice steady. "No matter what, I'm here for you."

Pranavi also made a new friend in Bangalore, Divyanka, who added a spark of positivity to her days. Together, they explored the city, shared stories, and helped each other navigate their internships.

Though life brought its challenges and complications, Pranavi and Aaditya's bond endured, proving that some connections, no matter how tested, remain unbreakable.

After returning from Bangalore, Pranavi found that everything had changed in Gurgaon. The familiar campus, the people, and even the atmosphere seemed different. It was as though the warmth she once felt had been replaced by a subtle chill. Struggling to adjust, she confided in Aaditya, who, as always, had a way of easing her mind.

"Pranavi," he said during one of their calls, "change isn't always bad. It just takes time to adjust. You've handled so much already—you'll handle this too. And don't forget, you're not alone in this."

His words, laced with encouragement, helped her navigate the unfamiliar dynamics. Aaditya had a way of influencing her thoughts, gently guiding her to find balance. Yet, despite his support, their friendship retained its usual spark of playful bickering.

One evening, as they argued over something trivial, Aaditya chuckled and said, "You know, it's hard for me to gulp even one morsel of food in a day without fighting with you."

Pranavi couldn't help but laugh. "That's because you're impossible to deal with," she retorted, though her voice carried more affection than irritation.

Their banter was constant, yet it was what made their bond special. Every day, one of them would call the other to share the little happenings of their lives, what they ate, who annoyed them, and what made them smile. Their friendship wasn't perfect, but it was unshakable.

On the other hand, things with Rohit had taken a bitter turn. Pranavi learned that he had been spreading rumors about her, claiming that she had "led him on" and was now avoiding him as though nothing had happened. The accusations stung deeply.

One afternoon, she sat alone, replaying the moments in her mind. "Was it a mistake to accept his friendship?" she wondered, her heart heavy.

Pranavi confided in a close friend, expressing her regret and hurt. "I never wanted this, you know? I thought we were friends. How could he twist things like this?"

Despite Rohit's attempts to tarnish her reputation, no one gave the rumors any weight. Her friends and classmates knew her character too well to believe such lies.

"Pranavi," one of her friends assured her, "don't let his words get to you. We all know you, and we know you're not capable of what he's saying. He's just bitter. That's on him, not you."

Though relieved by their trust, Pranavi couldn't shake the sadness that lingered. Her heart ached at the thought of what had once been a simple friendship now reduced to hostility.

But as always, Aaditya was her anchor. Whenever she felt overwhelmed, she turned to him.

"It's like I can't catch a break, Aaditya," she admitted during one of their late-night calls. "Everything feels so messy."

"It's just a phase, Pranavi," he replied, his voice steady and reassuring. "Don't let people like Rohit dim your light. You're better than that, and you have so many people who care about you. Focus on them. On us."

His words reminded her of her strength and the importance of holding on to the people who truly mattered. Despite the challenges, Pranavi began to find her footing again, with Aaditya's unwavering support lighting her path forward.

Chapter 11

Unsaid Words, Unfolding Paths

Meanwhile, Pranavi managed to secure a job. Though it wasn't her dream role, she was grateful for the opportunity and threw herself into the work, determined to make something of it despite the struggles she faced in her career. The first person she wanted to share the news with was Aaditya. By then, Aaditya was based in Kolkata.

She called him, her voice brimming with excitement. "Aaditya! I got a job!"

He paused, then replied warmly, "That's amazing, Pranavi! I'm so proud of you. I knew you'd make it. You deserve this and so much more."

Their conversations continued, though less frequently now. Their lives were beginning to stretch in different directions, but those brief exchanges remained a lifeline for Pranavi. They tethered her to a comfort that had once been her daily reality.

One day, news arrived that her former roommate from Bangalore, Sara, was getting married—in Kolkata. Pranavi was overjoyed. She had shared a deep bond with Sara during their internship, and this wedding gave her another reason to smile: the chance to finally meet Aaditya after so long.

Her heart fluttered at the thought. She began to daydream about their reunion—the warmth in his eyes, the jokes they'd share, the stories they'd exchange. She packed her bags with anticipation, accompanied by her brother Nabarghya, her forever anchor.

When they arrived in Kolkata, she wasted no time. She dialed Aaditya's number, heart racing.

"Hey, Aaditya! I'm in Kolkata! Let's meet up. It's been ages!"

His tone was polite but distant. "Oh, hey, Pranavi. I'm really tied up with work right now. Let me check my schedule and get back to you."

Disappointment tiptoed in, but she brushed it aside. He'd make time—he always had before. Days passed. Her phone remained silent.

Finally, on her last day in the city, she called again.

"Aaditya, it's my last day here. Can we meet, even for a short while?"

He hesitated, then replied, "I'm sorry, Pranavi. I'm really busy. I don't think I can make it."

That one line shattered every imagined moment. It wasn't just a refusal—it was the absence of effort. The weight of his words sank like a stone in her heart.

Nabarghya, having witnessed her hopeful anticipation turn into silent heartbreak, couldn't hold back anymore. As they packed to leave, he sat beside her.

"Didi, I know how you feel about him... but maybe it's time to let go. He's not meeting you halfway. This isn't fair to you."

Pranavi turned to him, tears brimming. "I've tried, Baba... I've tried so hard. But how do I just stop? He's been everything to me. I don't know how to undo this."

Nabarghya gently placed a hand on her shoulder. "I get it. But you deserve someone who chooses you—consistently, completely. Don't lose yourself waiting for someone who won't look back."

Though his words rang true, Pranavi's heart wasn't ready to obey. As they boarded their flight back to Delhi, she stared out the window, the skyline of Kolkata fading away.

Aaditya had distanced himself—but her feelings remained, quietly resilient, refusing to fade.

At one point, Pranavi found herself confronting a truth she couldn't ignore: her feelings for Aaditya had grown beyond friendship. What began as casual chats had evolved into something deeper, more delicate. But with that realization came fear.

The once-effortless calls now felt daunting. Each message she typed and erased, each phone call she hesitated to make, was a battle of emotions.

"What if I disturb him? What if he thinks I'm annoying?" her thoughts spiraled.

It wasn't without cause. Aaditya had always been kind, always made her feel special. The way he reassured her with a gentle hand on hers, the softness in his voice when she was hurting, the quiet understanding in his eyes—it all made her heart believe in something more.

And then there was his smile. That boyish, innocent smile that lit up everything around him. That smile alone had the power to calm every storm inside her.

But reality? It stood tall.

Aaditya had a girlfriend. A girl who, in Pranavi's eyes, was everything she wasn't—charming, confident, beautiful. They looked perfect together.

"She's smart... she fits into his world," Pranavi told herself. "He's made the right choice."

Still, her heart didn't listen.

That night, in the quiet of her room, her thoughts turned into a dialogue with her own heart:

Inner Voice: "Why are you doing this to yourself? You know this can't happen. He's already with someone else."

Pranavi (whispering): "I know... but I can't control how I feel. Every time I see him, everything else fades away."

Inner Voice (stern): "And what does it leave you with? Pain? Silence? Do you want that?"

Pranavi (pleading): "I don't want this. I just wish... I could stop. But how can I? He's the only one who listens, who understands."

Inner Voice (softly): "Then keep what you have. A beautiful friendship. Don't let love ruin the one thing that's always held you together."

Pranavi (hesitant): "But what if I can't hide it anymore? What if he finds out?"

Inner Voice: "He doesn't need to know. Focus on what you can control—his happiness, your friendship. Isn't that love too?"

A tear slid down her cheek as she hugged her pillow tightly.

Pranavi (softly): "It is... and I'll protect it. I'll protect us, even if it breaks me."

Her wish was simple: that Aaditya would always be near her. That no matter where life took them, they would face it together. But deep within, she knew—love wasn't always about receiving. Sometimes, love was choosing silence. Choosing strength. Choosing the happiness of the one you loved.

"He's my dear friend," she reminded herself. "And I'll hurt myself a thousand times over before I let anyone hurt him."

And so, she lived with her quiet truth, tucking her feelings in the corners of her heart, hoping they'd never spill over.

As the final year wound to a close, the campus buzzed with placement talks. Excitement filled the air, but Pranavi found herself sinking. She had tried hard, prepared relentlessly, yet no big company came forward with an offer. The placement coordinator's vague promises only added to the mounting frustration.

Feeling disillusioned but refusing to give up, Pranavi made a bold decision: she moved to Pune in search of better opportunities. The city was unfamiliar, but it whispered hope. Still, uncertainty clung to her like fog.

"Why does life always test me like this?" she thought. "Whenever I care, I lose. Whenever I hope, I fall."

Her life had become a pattern—attachment, loss, silence. But something inside her still kept moving, one trembling step at a time.

It was then that she received a call from Vivaan, the friend who had always watched over her like a big brother.

"Pranavi," he said gently, "I think you should know—Aaditya and his girlfriend have broken up. It wasn't working. The distance, the misunderstandings… it finally ended."

Pranavi froze. A part of her felt light, another felt burdened.

"There's more," he continued. "Some people think you had a role to play in this... because Aaditya spent so much time talking to you."

Her heart dropped.

"Vivaan, I never meant to... I never wanted any of this," she whispered. "I don't want to hurt anyone, especially not him."

She hung up, torn between guilt and hope. For the first time, she allowed herself to wonder—*could there really be something more between them?*

But life wasn't done testing her. A full month passed in Pune with no job offer. No callbacks. No breakthroughs.

"Not everyone gets what they want," she whispered to herself one night, hope flickering like the last candle in a storm.

She returned to Gurgaon, a little more bruised, a little more quiet. She completed her post-graduation soon after, but the road ahead remained foggy.

Now, she placed her trust in two things: God and her mother.

"No more dreams," she murmured. "Just steps. One at a time."

Her journey wasn't about happy endings. It was about enduring. About rising even when hope ran thin. And in that quiet, unseen courage - Pranavi moved forward.

Interlude: The Silent Goodbye

Some bonds don't break with thunder.

They wither quietly—like a flower that bloomed out of season, and knew it wouldn't last.

Pranavi once believed that the purest relationships are the ones where you can be your most unguarded self—where silence feels like home and not a void. With Aaditya, she had tasted that sense of belonging. He had been her safe space, her reflection, her rhythm in chaos.

But love, even in its purest form, cannot thrive on hope alone.

Like the rivers that change course over time, their bond, too, had shifted. It was no longer the effortless dance it once was. The calls were fewer, the silences longer. And though her heart waited at every crossroad, he never looked back.

Letting go of Aaditya was not a moment—it was a thousand moments breaking inside her.

It was her hand, hovering above the "call" button and retreating.

It was her smile dimming when someone mentioned his name.

It was looking through old photos and whispering to herself, *"We were happy once, weren't we?"*

She didn't hate him. She couldn't.

What they had was real—even if it was brief.

But love, no matter how fierce, must eventually surrender to self-respect.

"He will always mean something to me," she murmured one evening, staring out of the window as the city lights blurred into her tears.

"But perhaps... that chapter has closed. And I must now learn how to be whole, even with a page missing."

Pranavi wasn't choosing indifference.

She was choosing **peace**.

She was choosing **herself**.

Because sometimes, the most profound form of love… is learning when to stop chasing, and start healing.

At one point, Pranavi found herself confronting a truth she couldn't ignore, her feelings for Aaditya had grown beyond friendship. She had started liking him, but with this realization came a whirlwind of confusion and hesitation. The once-easy calls and messages now felt like monumental tasks. Her hands trembled each time she reached for her phone, her mind racing with thoughts like, "What if I disturb him? What if he finds me annoying?"

This change wasn't without reason. It was Aaditya's behavior that stirred her emotions - the way he held her hand during moments of reassurance, the gentle tone in his voice when he spoke to her, the way his eyes seemed to hold a thousand unspoken words when they met hers. And then there was his smile, that effortless, heartwarming smile that made Pranavi forget all her worries, even if just for a moment.

Despite the dreams that began to take root in her heart, Pranavi fought to keep her emotions in check. She reminded herself constantly of the reality that loomed large, Aaditya had a girlfriend. A girl who, in Pranavi's eyes, was everything Aaditya deserved.

"She's so beautiful, smart, and intelligent," Pranavi thought to herself. **"They look perfect together. He's made the right choice."**

But as she sat in the quiet of her room one evening, her inner turmoil grew louder.

Inner Voice: "Why are you doing this to yourself, Pranavi? You know this can't happen. He's already with someone else."

Pranavi (whispering to herself): "I know… but I can't control how I feel. Every time I see him, everything else fades away. I can't help it."

Inner Voice (sternly): "But you'll only end up hurting yourself. Is that what you want? To feel this pain every day?"

Pranavi (pleading): "I don't want to feel this way! I wish I could stop… but how can I? He's the only one who understands me, who listens without judgment."

Inner Voice (softening): "Then keep it as it is—a beautiful friendship. Don't let these feelings ruin what you already have."

Pranavi (hesitating): "But… what if I can't hide it? What if he finds out?"

Inner Voice: "He doesn't have to find out. You're stronger than this. Focus on what you can control—your friendship, his happiness. Isn't that what matters most to you?"

Pranavi sighed, hugging a pillow tightly as tears pricked her eyes.

Pranavi (quietly): "It is... it always has been. I'll protect our friendship, no matter what it costs me."

In her heart, Pranavi wished Aaditya could always be near her. She wanted him to stay by her side in every situation, whether life threw joy or adversity their way. But even as this silent wish grew stronger, she resolved to never let her feelings jeopardize their bond.

"He's my dear friend," she reminded herself. "And I'll hurt myself a thousand times over before I let anyone hurt him."

For now, Pranavi embraced their connection for what it was—a beautiful friendship that brought light to her life, even as her unspoken love for him lingered quietly in the shadows.

The end of college days marked the beginning of uncertainty for Pranavi. The campus buzzed with excitement as everyone was busy with placements, but for her, the experience was becoming increasingly disheartening. Despite her efforts, she hadn't secured a position with a good company, and the empty promises from the Placement Coordinator only added to her frustration.

Feeling dejected but determined to keep trying, Pranavi decided to move to Pune in search of better opportunities. The city offered a glimmer of hope, though she wasn't sure what awaited her there. Her mind wrestled with familiar doubts.

"Why does life always have to be this way?" she thought. **"Every time I hope for something good, the opposite happens. Whatever I wish for never comes true."**

Her life seemed to follow a cruel pattern: whenever she opened her heart and cared deeply for someone, life found a way to take them away. Yet, she continued to hope, despite knowing the pain it brought.

While navigating the job hunt in Pune, Pranavi received a call that caught her off guard. It was Vivaan, a close friend who was like an elder brother to her.

"Pranavi," Vivaan began, his tone serious, **"there's something you need to know about Aaditya."**

Her heart skipped a beat at the mention of his name.

"He's going through a rough patch," Vivaan continued. **"He broke up with his girlfriend. Things weren't working out between them, especially with her being in Mumbai and him in Gurgaon."**

Pranavi felt a wave of conflicting emotions wash over her - part relief, part guilt, and part sadness.

"But there's something else," Vivaan added hesitantly. **"Some people think you might've played a part in this. They're saying it's because of how much time Aaditya spends talking to you."**

Pranavi froze. She hadn't thought her late-night conversations and endless chats with Aaditya could be seen as anything more than the bond they shared. A part of her felt a flicker of happiness - could this mean there was a chance for something more between them? But another part of her was riddled with guilt.

"Vivaan," she finally said, her voice soft, **"I never meant for this to happen. I don't want to hurt anyone, especially not him."**

The conversation left her with a renewed sense of hope but also a deep unease. For the first time, she allowed herself to dream of the possibility that Aaditya might consider taking their friendship a step further.

Back in Pune, life continued to test her patience. She spent a month tirelessly searching for job opportunities but came up empty-handed.

"Not everyone gets what they want," she thought, her hope flickering like a candle in the wind. She returned to Gurgaon, feeling defeated but resigned. A few months later, Pranavi completed her post-graduation, yet her path remained uncertain.

By now, she had left everything in the hands of God and her mother.

"Why hope for anything?" she whispered to herself one night. **"Nothing I've ever wished for has come true."**

Pranavi decided to take life as it came, no longer chasing dreams or expectations. She braced herself for whatever life had in store for her, moving forward not out of hope, but out of sheer resilience. This was her life - a journey shaped by twists, turns, and the quiet strength of taking one step at a time.

Meanwhile, Pranavi managed to secure a job. Though it wasn't her dream role, she was grateful for the opportunity and threw herself into the work, determined to make something of it despite the struggles she faced in her career. The first person she wanted to share the news with was Aaditya. Aaditya then was based in Kolkata.

She called him, her excitement barely contained. **"Aaditya! I got a job!"** she exclaimed. **"It's not exactly what I dreamed of, but it's a start."**

His response warmed her heart. **"That's amazing, Pranavi! I'm so proud of you. I knew you'd make it. You deserve this and so much more."**

From then on, they continued to talk whenever their busy schedules allowed, their conversations weaving moments of joy and familiarity into their otherwise hectic lives. For Pranavi, those exchanges were a lifeline, keeping their bond alive despite the growing distance between them.

One day, news reached her that her former roommate from Bangalore, Sara, was getting married in Kolkata. Pranavi had shared a close bond with Sara during her stay in Bangalore, and the invitation brought a wave of happiness. But what thrilled her more was the thought of meeting Aaditya after a long time.

As soon as she received the invitation, Pranavi started dreaming about their meeting in Kolkata. She imagined catching up with Aaditya, sharing stories, and rekindling the bond they had built over years. Excitement bubbled within her as she packed her bags, preparing to fly to Kolkata with her brother, Nabarghya.

Nabarghya was more than just a sibling; he was her confidant, her pillar of strength. Always patient and caring, he knew Pranavi better than anyone else and stood by her through every high and low.

When they reached Kolkata, Pranavi wasted no time. She called Aaditya, her heart racing as she dialed his number.

"Hey, Aaditya!" she said, her voice brimming with excitement. **"I'm in Kolkata! Let's meet up. It's been ages since we've seen each other."**

Aaditya's tone was polite but distant. **"Oh, hey, Pranavi. I'm really tied up with work right now. Let me check my schedule, and I'll get back to you."**

Though his response dampened her excitement slightly, Pranavi clung to the hope that he would make time. Over the next few days, she waited eagerly for his call, imagining how their meeting would unfold.

As her trip neared its end, she called Aaditya again to check if he was free.

"Aaditya, it's my last day here. Can we meet up for even a little while?"

His reply shattered her expectations. **"I'm sorry, Pranavi. I'm really busy. I don't think I can make it."**

The weight of his words sank into her heart like a stone. He had turned down her proposal to meet and, worse, seemed to be ignoring her entirely.

Nabarghya, who had been silently observing his sister's anticipation and subsequent heartbreak, couldn't stay quiet. As they prepared to leave Kolkata, he sat beside her and gently said, **"Pranavi, I know how you feel about Aaditya. But... maybe it's time to let go. This isn't fair to you. He's not meeting you halfway."**

Pranavi looked at him, her eyes brimming with tears.

"I can't help it, Baba," she said, her voice barely above a whisper. **"I've tried... but I can't avoid him. He's been such an important part of my life. How do I just... let him go?"**

Her brother sighed, placing a reassuring hand on her shoulder. **"I understand, Didi. But sometimes, holding on only hurts more. You deserve someone who values you just as much as you value them."**

Though his words made sense, Pranavi couldn't bring herself to follow them. Aaditya was woven too deeply into her thoughts, her memories, her heart. As they boarded the flight back to Delhi, she couldn't shake the ache in her chest. Even though Aaditya had distanced himself, her feelings for him remained steadfast, leaving her caught in the painful grip of unrequited love.

Relationships, like rivers, have their own ebb and flow. They begin with a spark, a connection that feels unshakable, as though nothing could ever tarnish the bond. But as time passes, circumstances change, people change, and the once-clear waters of that connection become muddied by distance, misunderstandings, or the sheer weight of life.

Letting go of someone who once meant everything is one of life's greatest challenges. It's not just about releasing the person - it's about mourning the memories, the dreams, and the version of yourself that existed with them.

For Pranavi, her relationship with Aaditya was once a sanctuary. He had been her confidant, her anchor, the one who made her laugh even on her darkest days. Now, the thought of him slipping away felt like losing a part of herself.

But relationships, no matter how beautiful, can't thrive on one person's efforts alone. They require reciprocity, mutual care, and a willingness to walk side by side. Pranavi realized that letting go wasn't about erasing Aaditya from her life - it was about accepting that their bond had changed and releasing the expectations that tethered her to him.

"He will always mean something to me," she whispered one evening. **"But maybe it's time to rebuild myself while holding onto the love and lessons he gave me."**

Letting go doesn't mean weakness. Sometimes, it's the bravest act of self-love. Pranavi knew the journey ahead would be long and filled with moments of doubt, but she also knew she owed it to herself to try.

To Be Continued...

A few lines from the girl herself:

"I am not beautiful, but my heart carries a beauty of its own - a heart that knows how to knit delicate dreams, how to love deeply, care unconditionally, understand quietly, and trust with unwavering faith.

Every day, every moment, there's this endless search - a longing for someone who will come, take my hand, and never let go. Once, I thought I had found him. I felt his touch, his presence, and the warmth of that connection. For a fleeting moment, I believed my search was over.

But suddenly, it was gone - snatched away as if someone had erased that chapter from my story. I searched for him everywhere, in every corner of my heart, in every shadow of my life. I held onto my dream, hoping to reclaim what was lost. But when I opened my eyes, I realized the storm had taken him away from me.

And now, my life - *my life* - has turned into a barren desert, scorching and merciless, with nothing but thorns piercing my every step. I cry. I plead. But it's all in vain. Life, it seems, has played a cruel game with me."

Chapter 12

Becoming Her Own North Star

The air in Delhi was thick with heat, but Pranavi felt colder than ever. After returning from Kolkata, after the unanswered calls, after the silence she never expected from Aaditya—there was something in her that had quietly broken. She carried it with grace, like she always did, tucked behind her soft smiles and gentle nods, but it was there. A hollow space where hope once bloomed.

Work had begun, and though it wasn't the kind of role that set her heart racing, it was something. Something to pour herself into. Something to fill the hours, the days, the ache. Pranavi threw herself into her job with a kind of quiet desperation, showing up early, staying back late, learning more than was expected, saying less than what she felt.

The world didn't pause for heartbreak, and neither did she.

But every now and then, her fingers would hover above her phone screen, her heart foolishly whispering, "Maybe he missed me too... maybe he tried calling and just couldn't reach me."

He hadn't.

The silence from Aaditya was now a permanent soundtrack in her life. And for the first time in years, Pranavi found herself truly alone. Not lonely - no, she had friends, colleagues, her ever-loving mother, and her brother Nabarghya. But Aaditya had been the one she shared every shade of her day with, and now, even the brightest moments felt muted.

After her visit to Kolkata and the emotional storm that followed, Pranavi tried to slip back into the rhythm of her life in Gurgaon — showing up to work, replying to emails, attending meetings. Everything on the surface seemed to be functioning just fine. But inside, her soul was battered. She was slowly fading, emotionally and now, physically.

One morning, her body gave up.

Her vision blurred, her hands trembled, and her knees collapsed beneath her. Her brother rushed her to the hospital. Within moments, the sterile walls of a hospital room replaced the chaotic buzz of her daily routine.

The doctors wore worried expressions, and tests came back with warnings. It was critical — a possible life-or-death situation, they said.

Pranavi, even in her disoriented state, refused the idea of a blood transfusion. Not because she was scared, but because she was exhausted. Somewhere deep inside, she wondered if it would be easier to just... let go.

The doctors pleaded with her brother. "We need your consent. We don't have time."

Frantic, her brother dialed their mother. Without a second thought, her mother caught the next available flight and rushed to Delhi, her heart pounding louder than the engine of the plane she boarded.

As fate would have it, Aaditya got to know.

And he came. Quietly. Without announcement.

He told his family he had to explore job opportunities in Delhi — but that wasn't true. He came for her.

Their families already knew one another. Aaditya's mother adored Pranavi — she had once told her, "You're like the daughter I never had."

When Aaditya walked into the hospital room and saw her frail frame, something shifted. He sat beside her, held her hand like old times, and stayed with her family like he belonged there. Pranavi's mother, though overwhelmed, found solace in his presence.

But Pranavi... she didn't know what to feel. Was this care? Was this guilt? Was it love?

"I'll stay until you're better," Aaditya promised, his eyes serious, his voice gentle.

And he did. He stayed. Through the transfusions, through the sleepless nights, through the hospital corridors filled with echoes of silent prayers.

They came back to her flat in Delhi.

A Moment Between Breaths

It was a quiet evening in the small Delhi flat. The pale orange light of dusk filtered through the curtains, casting long, dreamy shadows across the walls. The room smelled faintly of antiseptic and tulsi, a mix of hospital memory and home comfort.

Pranavi lay on the bed, fragile and worn out, her body still fighting its battles. Her mother had just stepped out to get medicines — a small window of silence, unexpected and rare.

Aaditya sat by her bedside, sipping tea, his eyes flicking between his phone and her pale face.

She turned to him, her voice barely a whisper, "Why did you come, really?"

He looked at her — really looked — and set the cup down. For a long moment, he said nothing. The air between them was thick with words unspoken.

Then, without answering her question, he reached for her hand. His fingers, warm and trembling slightly, wrapped around hers with a gentleness that undid her.

"You scared me," he said quietly. "When I heard... I thought I'd lost you."

Pranavi blinked, unsure if she had imagined those words. Her lips parted to say something, but nothing came out.

And then, in the stillness of that moment — no visitors, no machines beeping, no mother hovering with concern — Aaditya leaned in, gently tucked a strand of hair behind her ear, and whispered, "You have no idea how much you matter."

It wasn't a confession. It wasn't a promise. It was something in between — something more honest than both.

For a second, everything disappeared — the betrayal that was to come, the silence that would follow, the heartbreak that was quietly waiting its turn.

In that fragile space, time softened its edges. It was just the two of them — a boy with haunted eyes and a girl whose heart still dared to hope.

He didn't kiss her. He didn't have to.

His silence, his touch, the way he looked at her — it said more than any words could.

When her mother returned, the moment dissolved like mist. They never spoke about it again.

But it stayed with Pranavi. Like a pressed flower between the pages of her life — delicate, faded, and unforgettable.

And when she was stable enough to go back home, he told her softly, "I'll see you again soon."

He never did.

Pranavi's mother took her back to their hometown — determined to bring her daughter back to life, not just in body, but in spirit. Pranavi resigned from her job. She was too broken to continue. Her mother cooked her favorite meals, took her on morning walks, stayed by her side like a shadow of unconditional love.

In between sips of soup and long silences, Pranavi tried to reach out to Aaditya. A message. A call. A word passed through a friend.

Nothing.

He disappeared. Just like that.

And with him, disappeared the last shred of hope she'd been clutching onto.

She stood by the window of her childhood room one evening, holding her phone to her chest, the screen blank, her inbox empty.

A whisper escaped her lips —

"So this is how it ends... Not with a goodbye. Just silence."

A silence that echoed louder than any heartbreak ever had.

Chapter 13

The House That Healed Her

After days of medical uncertainty and emotional weight, Pranavi was finally well enough to travel. Her mother didn't think twice - she took her home, to where the earth smelled of rain, memories, and the healing arms of family.

The house in her hometown wasn't extravagant, but it was sacred - a place stitched together with generations of love, sacrifice, and stories whispered under mosquito nets.

Here, everyone moved around her like sunlight - her mother, her pillar of unshakable care, cooked her favorite meals, fed her with her own hands, measured her pulse more often than the doctors did. She stayed up late, watching her daughter breathe, afraid to blink.

Hoping a change of environment would cheer her up, Pranavi's mother took her and her brother to her maternal aunt's house — a place filled with warmth, laughter, and comforting memories.

Her maternal aunt - *mahi*, as she fondly called her - became the second heartbeat in that house. Mahi, who had never had children of her own, had poured all her maternal love into Pranavi and Nabarghya since they were born. Her presence was not a duty — it was devotion. She massaged Pranavi's frail legs with warm mustard oil, narrated silly jokes just to coax a smile, and sang lullabies from her own childhood.

"You know," Mahi would say, sitting at her bedside while braiding her hair, "when you were little, I would pray that if I ever had a daughter, she would be exactly like you. But then I stopped praying. I realized... God had already sent you to me."

Those words, soft as a breeze, stayed with Pranavi - they were balm to her aching heart.

Her grandmother, too, held a place that no one else could. Old, wrinkled, and wise, she had a voice like a folk song - slow, sweet, and filled with emotion. Every night, Pranavi would sleep beside her, resting her head on the curve of her grandmother's shoulder, like she used to do as a child.

Under the dim glow of a hurricane lamp, her grandmother would speak of other worlds - of her youth, of being the daughter of a royal family, of lavish feasts and silken sarees... and how marriage had brought her into a more modest life, where resilience replaced luxury.

"But child," her grandmother once said, stroking Pranavi's hair, "real royalty is not in what you wear. It's in how you walk through storms and still smile at the rain."

Pranavi's eyes had welled up then. These weren't just bedtime stories. These were blueprints of courage — her mother's, her grandmother's, her aunt's — passed down through love and lived truths.

Surrounded by their unwavering strength, something within her began to heal.

She had been shattered in places even she couldn't name, but these women — these warriors cloaked in sarees and simplicity — were slowly stitching her together again, not with thread, but with presence.

For once, she didn't have to explain her silence. She didn't have to hide her pain behind smiles.

Here, love wasn't loud. It didn't need to be. It was in the way her mother brought her tea exactly the way she liked it, in the way her aunt hummed old songs while folding laundry, in the way her grandmother ran her fingers through her hair as she drifted to sleep.

In this home built of stories, tears, and love that asked for nothing in return — Pranavi remembered who she was before the heartbreak, before the hospital, before the silence from Aaditya.

And slowly, she began to return to herself.

One evening, after a long, exhausting day at work, she sat by the window of her rented apartment, staring at the blurred neon lights outside. The city felt unfamiliar. Or maybe it was she who had become unfamiliar to herself.

She opened her journal and began to write - something she hadn't done in months.

"I want to stop looking back. But how do you erase someone who feels like home? How do you stop missing someone who was once your mirror? And how do you forgive yourself for believing they'd stay?"

Her pen paused, ink pooling against paper.

"Maybe this pain is my passage. Maybe heartbreak isn't a dead end but a doorway. Maybe I'm supposed to become my own North Star."

She closed the journal and breathed, for the first time in weeks, without a lump in her throat.

Days passed. Then weeks.

One morning, her phone buzzed with an unknown number. It was one of her Ex-Managers. A position had opened up in a rising startup that aligned with her aspirations - strategy, creativity, leadership.

She interviewed. She got selected.

She called her mother first. Then her brother. She didn't even consider calling Aaditya. That chapter was no longer hers to revisit.

In her new role, she began to shine again. The confidence that had once flickered now returned as fire. She was mentoring others, presenting to clients, handling deadlines like a storm. And yet, the gentleness in her never left. She led with empathy, with the quiet strength of someone who had known loss, loved deeply, and chosen to rise anyway.

One day, she came across a message request on social media. It was from Aaditya.

"Hey... I heard about your new role. Congratulations. I'm really happy for you. Hope you're doing well."

She stared at the message for a long while.

She didn't reply.

Not out of spite. But because she had outgrown the version of herself that waited.

Some people are meant to be memories. And some memories are meant to remind us how far we've come.

That night, Pranavi looked into the mirror.

Her reflection didn't look for validation anymore. Her smile didn't wait for someone to understand it.

She had become her own home.

Her own light.

Her own North Star.

Chapter 14

The Echo of Goodbye

Time passed, but something inside Pranavi had shifted. Life was no longer about chasing dreams - it had become about surviving moments. Each day, she woke up, put on a brave face, and went through the motions. She smiled at colleagues, laughed at silly jokes, and shared cups of tea with acquaintances who barely knew her heart. To the world, she looked like someone who had it all together - a strong, independent woman carving her space in a chaotic world.

But inside, she was breaking.

In the silence of her rented room, far away from her family, she often found herself whispering to the walls. There were nights when she would lie awake, watching the fan rotate in slow circles above her bed, wondering if anyone truly saw her. Her voice had grown softer.

Her spirit quieter. The once vibrant, lively girl was slowly learning the art of becoming invisible in a world that never truly asked her how she was doing.

She was all by herself, fighting the world.

She didn't want to be strong all the time. Deep within, she longed for someone she could lean on, someone to sit beside her and simply listen without asking questions or offering advice. She wished she could depend on someone. But there was no one. No familiar voice at the end of the day, no warm hand to hold during moments of doubt.

And so, she did it all herself.

Every bill paid, every decision made, every emotion buried with care - she did it without help. Every time life threw a challenge her way, she faced it alone. Her loneliness wasn't always loud, but it was there in the way she lingered a little longer in coffee shops, hoping for a conversation, or in the way she sometimes laughed too hard at her own jokes, just to fill the silence.

And yet, this solitude made her stronger - day by day, moment by moment.

She began to accept that maybe this was how her life was meant to unfold. Maybe there was never going to be someone who would walk beside her in this journey. Maybe, this was what God had planned for her: a life of quiet courage and relentless strength. She watched people holding hands, sitting close, whispering secrets to each other while she walked alone on the same roads, unnoticed.

There were evenings when she would sit by the window and simply watch the world pass by. Strangers laughing. Friends meeting. Lovers embracing. And there she was - just her and her thoughts.

People outside thought she was the happiest person alive. After all, she wore her cheer like a well-fitted garment. She cracked jokes, helped others, excelled at work, and always seemed to have the right words. But inside, she was crumbling.

Her soul screamed for comfort, for understanding. Her heart ached to be held.

But no one saw that.

They saw her smile, not her sleepless nights. They admired her strength, not knowing it was forged in fire.

And yet, through it all, she endured.

Because somewhere deep inside her brokenness, there still lived a flicker of hope. Not for a perfect ending, but for the strength to carry on. For the belief that maybe, just maybe, even the most solitary paths can lead to unexpected places.

And for now, that belief was enough to keep her going.

One rainy evening in the heart of the city, when thunderclouds lingered like unspoken emotions, Pranavi and Shravani found themselves sitting under the tin roof of a tiny roadside tea stall — the kind only true locals knew. The air smelled of petrichor and boiling ginger tea, and for a while, the chaos of the world melted into the hush of falling rain.

Shravani passed Pranavi a cup, the steam curling between them like a silent promise of comfort. "You've changed," she said gently, her eyes searching Pranavi's face.

Pranavi smiled, a tired one. "I had to."

Shravani didn't speak for a while, just watched the droplets race down the edges of the roof. Then she said, "It's okay to be strong. But it's okay to miss the parts of you that were softer too."

Something in those words cracked open a space in Pranavi's chest. Not the kind that hurt — but the kind that reminded her that being seen was healing in itself.

They talked till the rain stopped, sharing not just stories, but the weight of what wasn't said. In that moment, beneath a humble tin roof in a forgotten corner of the city, they weren't just friends. They were each other's reminders — of home, of hope, and of the girl they never wanted to lose.

Chapter 15

The Stillness Between Storms

The heartbreak had passed like a storm, but in its wake, Pranavi was left with stillness — not peace, but the hollow silence that comes after chaos.

This time, she didn't try to fill it with calls or long messages. She didn't reach out or look back. She simply turned toward the only thing that had never failed her — her work.

Her job became her refuge, her escape, her battlefield, and her triumph.

From the moment she stepped into the office each morning, Pranavi immersed herself in tasks with quiet determination. She wasn't chasing praise. She wasn't trying to prove anything to the world. She was simply trying to rebuild — brick by brick, file by file, email by email.

Her calendar was full, her desk a map of post-its and spreadsheets, her mind tuned into KPIs and client deliverables. She volunteered for new projects, took on extra shifts, mentored interns — anything to keep her from feeling the void she carried within.

Her colleagues admired her, some envied her. "How do you manage it all?" they asked.

Pranavi would smile and say, "I like keeping busy."

But the truth was far more layered. Keeping busy meant she didn't have to think. It meant fewer reminders of Aaditya's silence, fewer chances for her heart to ache with the memories of what could have been.

She no longer waited for texts. No longer counted days between conversations. If he came, he came. If he didn't, she wasn't going to pause her life anymore.

She was learning how to live without him — and that, she realized, was the real milestone.

There were still lonely evenings, of course. Days when her eyes welled up without warning. Days when she'd see a message notification and her heart would leap — only to settle into quiet disappointment.

But they were fewer now.

She found joy in new things - a freshly brewed cup of coffee on a rainy morning, a compliment from her manager, a solo movie night, a book that made her cry and smile at the same time.

She started journaling again. Her words, once about him, were now about herself. Her hopes, her wins, her truths.

And somewhere in the rhythm of this new routine, Pranavi discovered something beautiful:

Her life didn't need to revolve around someone else's presence.

She could be the sun in her own sky.

Chapter 16

The City of Hills and Healing

Just when she thought she had found her rhythm in Gurgaon, a call changed everything.

It was from one of her former managers — a gentleman who had seen Pranavi's potential long before Pranavi had seen it in herself.

"There's a position opening up in Dehradun," her manager said. "It's a challenging role. New territory, a different culture. But I think you're ready for it."

The moment she heard the name *Dehradun*, something stirred within her — a strange, gentle flutter.

Mountains. Misty mornings. A slower life.

It felt like the universe was whispering, *Here's your fresh start.*

Within weeks, Pranavi packed her bags again. A new city. A new role. A new chapter.

Dehradun greeted her with open skies and quiet streets. The air smelled different — cleaner, calmer. The people were warm, unhurried. Her office was tucked away in a green part of town, where birdsong replaced traffic noise.

And for the first time in months, she didn't feel like she was running. She was simply... living.

She poured herself into her work again — but this time, it wasn't just an escape. It was a space of joy. Her team respected her, her ideas were heard, and slowly, she started building not just a reputation, but a new life.

Weeks turned into months.

She bought a car with her own hard-earned money — a milestone she once only dreamed of.

Every weekend, she would drive to the hills, windows rolled down, music floating into the breeze. And in those moments, she smiled — genuinely, softly. Not because she had forgotten the past. But because she was finally forgiving herself for it.

Maybe her manifestations were coming true.

Maybe this was what healing looked like — not loud or cinematic, but quiet, steady, and deeply personal.

Chapter 17

When the World Stood Still

The world had never known silence like this.

Streets that once bustled with life stood eerily empty. The skies, once streaked with aircraft trails and noise, now held only birdsong and a strange, unsettling quiet. It felt like time had paused — not to give people rest, but to confront them with a stillness they hadn't known how to handle.

The year was 2020.

The word "COVID" no longer sounded unfamiliar or far away. It had reached every corner of the globe, including the quaint hills of Dehradun, where Pranavi was living with her mother and brother.

The virus didn't just affect lungs. It seeped into people's hearts, their thoughts, their souls. It made strangers out of neighbours. It locked families behind closed doors. And worst of all, it took loved ones away before final goodbyes could be whispered.

Every time the television was turned on, it was a fresh dose of grief — endless images of crowded hospitals, tearful faces behind masks, and pyres burning in corners of cities that once celebrated life.

Pranavi, like everyone else, had no choice but to adjust. Her office moved into remote mode. Zoom calls replaced chai breaks. Daily stand-ups were now conducted in pyjamas. But underneath the surface of work and "new normals," something had shifted.

She was lucky — she knew it. She wasn't alone. She was in Dehradun, the city of hills and healing, tucked safely under the same roof with her mother and brother. And that made all the difference.

The three of them lived a simple routine. Morning prayers. Home-cooked meals. Long conversations over tea. The kind of moments people often missed in the rush of everyday life. The outside world was burning, breaking — but within their walls, they held each other close.

And yet, the grief of the world seeped in.

There were days when Pranavi would read the news and simply weep. For people she had never met. For lives she could not save. For the helplessness that wrapped itself around her chest like a vice.

One evening, as the three of them lit a diya in remembrance of those lost, her mother said softly, "This is a time God has sent to remind us what really matters. It's not work. Not money. Not even achievements. It's people. It's presence."

Pranavi nodded, tears streaming silently.

She began journaling again — not just her thoughts, but gratitude. Every morning she wrote one line - "I am alive. My family is safe." And that, she realized, was more than enough.

They played board games on weekends. Tried new recipes. Watched old family albums together. The walls of their home were filled with stories again.

Still, fear never fully left the room. Each sneeze was a jolt. Each phone call from a distant friend came with the dread of bad news.

But through it all, she held on — to faith, to the warmth of her family, and to the still, small voice inside her that whispered, *"You will come out stronger."*

COVID was not just a health crisis. It was an emotional reckoning.

It asked people to confront their loneliness, their fears, and their deepest regrets.

For Pranavi, it was also a quiet nudge — reminding her to live slowly, love fully, and to hold sacred the people who matter.

In a world that was grieving, her little family became her fortress.

And within that stillness, she began to understand something profound:

The greatest blessing is not in having everything, but in having someone to come home to — and the time to cherish them.

Chapter 18

When the World Stood Still

Just before the world began to shut down — before masks became our second skin, and silence cloaked the streets — something unexpected happened.

One evening, as the hills of Dehradun bathed in fading sunlight and the world outside slowly dimmed, Pranavi sat on her bed, aimlessly scrolling through Facebook. Her mother stirred dal in the kitchen while humming an old tune, her brother was absorbed in his laptop, and the gentle rustle of the pine trees outside her window was the only soundtrack to her thoughts.

And then — a notification.

"You have a new friend request."

A name she didn't immediately recognize. But it was the profile picture that made her pause.

A man, casually holding a guitar. A faint smile playing on his lips, like he had just strummed the last note of a song only he knew. There was something oddly familiar about his face — not just because it was expressive or warm — but because it felt like a déjà vu.

Curious, she tapped the profile.

And there it was — the connection.

He had once worked in the same company she was employed at. They hadn't interacted before, but now, during a time when the world was distancing itself, his presence felt strangely close.

Pranavi stared at the picture a little longer.

Something in his eyes held a softness, a calm. And that guitar — that carefree presence in a world brimming with anxiety — made her feel something she hadn't felt in a while.

Intrigue.

A flutter of curiosity.

Hope?

She didn't accept the request immediately. Her fingers hovered over the screen, caught in a battle between habit and heart. After all, she had made peace with solitude. Letting someone new in felt like undoing all the strength she had gathered piece by piece.

But still... that guitar.

It lingered in her thoughts even as she closed the app.

That evening, she sat on her balcony as dusk draped itself over the city, and wondered — *What if this is the universe's way of saying something? What if this is not just coincidence?*

She didn't message him. He hadn't sent one either.

But the seed had been planted.

Unseen. Quiet. Full of promise.

In a world shutting down, a door had quietly opened — not outside, but within.

Chapter 19

The Quiet Fulfillment

The air smelled faintly of incense and marigold. Soft murmurs of guests filled the room. Somewhere, a shehnai played — the kind of tune that wrapped itself around old hopes and new beginnings.

Pranavi sat quietly in the bridal chamber, wrapped in crimson and gold, but her thoughts wore softer colors — hues of memory, of laughter and tears, of moments that shaped the woman she had become.

There was no rush in her breath, no storm in her chest.

Just a stillness. A knowing.

As the mirror in front of her reflected the bride she had become, her eyes searched deeper — not for flaws, but for the girl she used to be.

That girl… she had once believed in fairytales. Then she learned how harsh life could be. She had watched friendships crumble, love vanish without explanation, and dreams take detours she never imagined.

She had once begged the universe for someone to walk beside her.

And yet, for years, she walked alone.

Until, slowly and quietly, life shifted.

Ayush had become a whisper that stayed. What began as casual conversations during lockdown grew into something gentle yet steady. He didn't try to fill the spaces Aaditya had left — instead, he created new ones, where healing could happen, where laughter returned, where Pranavi could be herself — unfiltered, unafraid.

He never rushed her. He never demanded explanations. He simply stayed.

In him, she had found not a prince, but a partner.

Not a perfect man, but a peaceful presence.

It wasn't the love story she had once imagined. There were no grand declarations, no cinematic surprises. Just real moments — phone calls during flu days, songs shared over texts, patient silences, understanding glances.

And perhaps, that's what made it perfect.

As the sound of footsteps grew louder, Pranavi stood up. Her mother peeked in, eyes moist, smile trembling — the woman who had been her fortress through everything.

"Ready?" she whispered, adjusting her dupatta like she had a hundred times before.

Pranavi nodded.

This time, she wasn't stepping into the unknown. She was walking toward something she had built — with time, with pain, with love that healed in slow rhythms.

The door opened, and as she took that first step forward, she carried within her every version of herself — the child who danced under Assam's rain, the girl who once loved silently, the woman who rose from every heartbreak, and the soul who had finally learned:

Sometimes, the best endings are the ones you don't see coming — not because they're loud, but because they arrive quietly… and stay.

A Letter from Pranavi to Her Younger Self

(To the girl who once sat in silence, waiting for life to make sense)

Dear Younger Me,

I know you're tired.

Tired of being strong, of wiping your own tears, of always understanding everyone else but never feeling understood.

I remember how you curled up at night, questioning your worth just because someone chose silence over honesty. I remember how you smiled through pain, thinking that if you just kept giving, maybe someone would stay.

You were always the girl who loved deeply — quietly, with all your heart.

You carried your father's values, your mother's resilience, and your brother's laughter.

You carried everyone's expectations too — and somewhere along the way, forgot to ask what *you* wanted.

You believed in forever...

Until forever ghosted you without a goodbye.

You searched for answers in empty inboxes, in unread messages, in half-smiles during college corridors.

And when you found none, you blamed yourself.

But let me tell you something, my love —

None of it was your fault.

Not the way he left.

Not the tears that followed.

Not the loneliness that lingered longer than it should have.

You were never too much. You were never not enough.

You were just... you.

And that was always beautiful.

I wish I could go back and hold you.

Tell you that the pain won't last forever, even if it feels like it will.

That one day, you'll walk into rooms without shrinking.

That one day, you'll buy your own car.

That one day, you'll walk down an aisle — not chasing love, but *welcoming* it.

And it will feel different.

Not like fireworks or storms — but like sunlight on skin. Like peace after a long night.

Ayush will come.

Not like the others — not loud or hurried — but like a melody you forgot you loved.

He won't fix you, no.

But he'll sit with you while you heal.

And he'll stay.

So, hold on a little longer.

Cry if you must, but keep going.

Because the woman you're becoming —

She's magic.

She's everything you once prayed for.

And she's writing this letter to tell you…

You made it.

With all my love,

Future You

For years, Pranavi had imagined different versions of this day. Some filled with tears, some with quiet farewells, and some that never arrived at all. But this one — this day — felt like it had gently walked up to her and whispered, "You're ready now."

Ayush was not someone who barged into her life. He had knocked gently. Patiently. He didn't try to fill her silences; he sat beside them. He didn't try to erase her past; he honored it. With him, love didn't come in a whirlwind. It arrived like early morning sunlight — soft, warming, and certain.

The ceremonies went by in a blur — laughter, sacred verses, turmeric-stained palms, smiling faces, and a whirlwind of colors. But the one moment that would stay etched in her memory forever was when their eyes met — right before the pheras began.

Ayush looked at her not with possession, but with quiet respect. As if he understood that the woman sitting beside him was made of stories — of wounds and wonder, of goodbyes and growing. And that to love her meant to honor every chapter she had lived before this one.

After the rituals, when the crowd thinned out and the stars took over the sky, they sat side by side — still in their wedding finery — on the terrace of her childhood home.

Ayush reached out, gently holding her hand.

"You've lived so much before me, Pranavi," he said softly, "but I want to walk every step with you from here on — at your pace, in your rhythm."

She looked at him, eyes brimming.

"I never thought I'd find someone... who would not just love me, but choose to understand me."

And in that moment, without declarations or grandeur, something within her finally exhaled.

Not because the past had vanished. Not because every scar was healed. But because, for the first time, she didn't have to hide any part of herself anymore.

She could be loved... just as she was.

Chapter 20

Morning Light

The first rays of sunlight tiptoed through the soft linen curtains of their hotel room in Udaipur. Outside, the gentle waters of Lake Pichola mirrored the orange blush of dawn, as if nature itself was waking slowly, reverently.

Inside the room, everything was hushed — as if the world had paused for just a little while to let two souls breathe in the beginning of forever.

Pranavi stirred beneath the sheets, the crisp morning air brushing against her face. She blinked open her eyes, unfamiliar with the feeling of waking up beside someone. Beside her, Ayush slept soundly — his face calm, his breathing steady, one arm loosely draped across her waist, as if even in sleep, he wanted her close.

She watched him for a moment, her heart swelling with something quiet yet infinite.

This wasn't the kind of love she had read about in books — full of drama and fireworks. This was something else entirely.

It was the warmth of two mugs of chai shared on a breezy balcony.

The way he tucked her hair behind her ear when she wasn't looking.

The way his presence, without saying a word, told her — *I'm here, and I'm not going anywhere.*

She slowly slipped out of bed, wrapping a shawl around her shoulders, and stepped onto the balcony. Below, the city of lakes was just beginning to stir. The faint sound of temple bells, a distant flute, birds circling in the golden sky — everything felt like it had been orchestrated to match her still heart.

Moments later, Ayush joined her.

His hair tousled, eyes soft from sleep, he stood behind her and placed his chin lightly on her shoulder.

"Penny for your thoughts?" he whispered.

She smiled faintly, eyes still on the lake.

"Just... trying to believe this is real."

Ayush didn't respond with words. He simply reached for her hand, laced his fingers through hers, and held on — as if to say, *It is.*

They stood there for a long time, not needing to speak. Not needing to fill the silence. For the first time in a long time, Pranavi's heart wasn't searching. It wasn't waiting or hoping or aching.

It was *home.*

And in that moment — with wind in her hair, sun on her face, and a promise wrapped around her hand — she finally understood:

Love doesn't always arrive with noise.

Sometimes, it tiptoes in with the morning light.

Chapter 21

The House That Chose Them

Before the keys were handed, before the dusty corners of their new home echoed with the sound of laughter and shifting furniture, there was *Dehradun* — a place that now held more than just hills and memory-laden air. It held *family*.

Ayush's hometown welcomed Pranavi like the daughter it had long been waiting for. His parents' warmth, the joyous chaos of extended family, the aroma of homemade food, and the old house filled with stories — it was all overwhelming, but in the gentlest of ways.

Everyone adored her — not just for who she was, but for the peace she carried within her. The way she helped in the kitchen, sat beside elders with genuine interest, laughed with the younger ones like she'd always been a part of their inside jokes — it left an imprint.

She had always believed in karma. In manifestations whispered at 11:11. In little promises made to the skies. And now... she stood at the threshold of her fulfilled wish.

"This feels unreal," she whispered to Ayush that night, sitting beneath the stars on his terrace. "Like I've stepped into a dream I'd written for someone else."

He gently pulled her closer. "Then stay in it with me, forever."

The next morning, as soft light bathed the hills, they went to the temple — *that* temple.

The one where Pranavi, once upon a time, had made a silent promise.

A promise whispered between tears and trembling hope — *"I'll come back here after my marriage with Ayush."*

And there she stood now, beside him, married, adored, glowing with gratitude. She folded her hands in reverence, eyes moist with fulfillment.

The priest smiled knowingly as if he saw something divine unfold.

After the prayer, Ayush took her hand and said, "Now, let me show you my world."

They roamed around the city like two love-drunk teenagers who couldn't keep their hands off each other. He showed her the places he once escaped to when the world got too loud — a quiet corner by the river, a chai shop tucked behind a school, an abandoned bus stop where he used to scribble thoughts in a notebook.

Every spot became theirs now. Every story got a new ending — one where she was part of the frame.

Their fingers intertwined like they'd never want to let go. They clicked polaroids, teased each other about the past, and sat on park benches just to watch the day pass slowly — together.

"I want to remember this," she said, resting her head on his shoulder.

"You will," he smiled. "Because we've only just begun."

And then came the keys.

Their *first* home — a new beginning, layered with old promises, silent prayers, and cosmic alignments.

It wasn't just a chapter. It was the chapter where all the previous ones made sense.

A home not just of cement and bricks, but of *answered prayers.*

A New Beginning in Banaras

Just a few days after the laughter-filled dinner, life, as it always does, gently nudged them toward the next chapter.

Ayush received the official call — his semester was about to begin, and it was time for him to return to Banaras, where he was a Professor at one of the most respected universities in the city. The air at home changed slightly, not with gloom, but with the quiet stirrings of transition.

"Are you ready for Banaras?" he asked Pranavi one evening, as they sipped tea on the balcony.

She looked up, her fingers curled around the warm cup. "I don't know... I'm excited. But I'm nervous too."

Banaras — a city dipped in history, tradition, and a kind of spiritual rhythm Pranavi hadn't yet experienced. It wasn't just a new address. It was a new life. New people, unfamiliar roads, different routines. And yet, it was also *his* world — a world she was ready to walk into, hand in hand with him.

[Scene: Their cozy bedroom, dimly lit. The clock ticks softly. Pranavi sits cross-legged on the bed, holding a diary. Ayush is standing by the window, looking out at the night sky. He turns around slowly.]

Ayush (softly):

"Are you scared?"

Pranavi (looks up, smiling faintly):

"A little... maybe more than I thought I would be."

Ayush (walks over, sits beside her):

"I know Banaras isn't exactly your comfort zone. It's dusty and chaotic and... very different from here."

Pranavi (nudging him playfully):

"So reassuring, Professor."

Ayush (grins, then gently takes her hand):

"But it's home. And now, it'll be ours. I'll make sure you don't feel out of place... not for even a second."

Pranavi (eyes softening):

"It's not the place that worries me, Ayush. It's the unknown. New routines, new people... being away from Maa, Nabarghya, everything I've known."

Ayush (pauses, looking into her eyes):

"You'll never be away from love, Pranu. That's coming with you — packed in your suitcase, tucked between every chapter of your story. I'll be right there... for every meltdown, every chai craving, every time you miss home."

Pranavi (smiles, a tear rolling down her cheek):

"You know, I used to think I'd have to walk this life alone. I'd built walls so high... and then you appeared with your guitar, a random Facebook request, and turned it all upside down."

Ayush (wipes her tear gently):

"And here I am, breaking those walls — brick by brick — just to build something new with you."

Pranavi (whispers):

"Promise me one thing?"

Ayush (nods):

"Anything."

Pranavi:

"When I feel lost, like I don't belong — just hold my hand and remind me that I do."

Ayush (tightens his grip on her hand):

"Always. Your hand is my compass now, and Banaras is just the next chapter. Together."

[They sit in silence, letting the moment sink in. Two hearts, one promise — to find home in each other no matter where life takes them.]

The next morning, her suitcase lay open on the bed, half-filled with sarees, books, and a diary she hadn't touched in months. As she packed, her mind whirled with thoughts — *Will I find work there? Will I make friends? Will I feel like I belong?*

But somewhere between the folds of her clothes and the scent of her favorite perfume, a thought gently settled in — *I have him. That's my beginning.*

Her mother-in-law came in, placing a hand on her shoulder, "Banaras will love you, beta. You carry light wherever you go."

The reassurance brought a faint smile. Pranavi knew the road ahead wouldn't be without bumps, but this time, she wasn't walking it alone.

As they loaded their bags into the car that would take them to the railway station, Ayush held her hand firmly, as if answering the questions she hadn't spoken aloud.

"We'll figure it out, one thing at a time. And I'll be right there — always."

As the train pulled out of the station, Dehradun slowly vanished into the distance, and with it, a hundred memories of their first few days as husband and wife. But ahead, Banaras awaited — chaotic, soulful, mysterious Banaras — and Pranavi, with all her strength, was ready to begin again.

Chapter 22

A New Beginning in Banaras

The laughter from the family dinner still lingered in Pranavi's ears as the car hummed down the road toward Banaras. Her fingers gently laced through Ayush's on the armrest — a quiet affirmation of their togetherness, and a silent comfort for the unknown ahead.

Banaras.

A city that echoed with history and whispered secrets through its ghats, where time didn't just pass — it lingered. For Ayush, this city was familiar, grounding, a return to his rhythm. For Pranavi, it was a blank canvas — beautiful, yes, but unfamiliar.

The morning they arrived, the city greeted them with golden sunlight filtering through neem trees and the far-off sound of conch shells. Pranavi stepped out of the car and looked around. Everything felt slower here, more deliberate, as though even the air moved with intention.

Their new home was nestled near Assi Ghat, modest but full of charm. Wooden windows framed the sunrise, and the balcony overlooked a stretch of rooftops and temple spires. Pranavi stood in the empty living room, her suitcase still zipped, and whispered to herself — "Let's make this a home."

In the days that followed, Banaras slowly revealed itself to her.

She woke up to temple bells, the scent of marigolds from street vendors, and the call of the chaiwala every morning. She wandered through narrow alleys where shops sold everything from bangles to brass lamps. The ghats were where she found her moments of stillness — women whispering prayers, children flying kites, and old sadhus sitting like timekeepers.

Every evening, Ayush returned home tired but content. He spoke of his students, of lectures that went longer than planned, of debates that stirred passion in young minds. And one afternoon, Pranavi visited his campus — stood at the back of the classroom, unnoticed at first.

Ayush was in his element. Confident, thoughtful, inspiring.

She watched him from the doorway, arms crossed, smiling softly.

"He belongs here," she thought. *"And maybe, if I try... I can belong here too."*

That evening, they walked by the Ganga. He pointed out the spot where he once used to come and sit during college days — a hidden ledge behind a banyan tree.

"It's peaceful here," Pranavi whispered, leaning into him.

He smiled. "This is the place I came to when I was figuring out life. And now, you're here. With me. I think life figured itself out."

They didn't need many words after that.

Later that night, in their small kitchen, they cooked together for the first time in their Banaras home. Pranavi chopped while Ayush stirred, music playing in the background, the scent of cumin filling the room. It was imperfect — they burnt the rotis — but it was *theirs*.

After dinner, they sat on the floor, sharing kheer and stories. Laughter echoed through the walls of their new home, and in that moment, it no longer felt unfamiliar.

Banaras wasn't just Ayush's city anymore. It was theirs.

And as the river flowed silently nearby, so did time — gently, steadily — carrying with it two people learning to build a life hand-in-hand.

It was a pause between heartbeats..

The golden evening sun bathed the ghats of Banaras in a soft, nostalgic hue. The Ganga flowed beside them, silent and sacred, its waters whispering ancient lullabies to the stone steps that had witnessed centuries of prayers, partings, and promises.

Ayush and Pranavi sat quietly, their hands intertwined, their feet just brushing the river's edge. It wasn't silence born of absence — it was a silence full of presence, of comfort, of knowing.

The kind that doesn't need words.

A breeze picked up, teasing the loose strands of Pranavi's hair, while Ayush tightened his hold just a little, a quiet gesture that said — *I see you. I'm here.*

She turned to him and smiled — the kind of smile that grows slowly from the heart, not forced, not hurried, just… real.

It had been a journey — the kind no story can truly capture in its entirety. From heartbreaks to healing, from quiet tears under city lights to whispered dreams in temple courtyards, Pranavi had lived many lifetimes within this one.

She had found love in the most unexpected of ways. Not through grand gestures or dramatic confessions, but in patient conversations, shared burdens, morning tea rituals, and the way Ayush looked at her when she wasn't watching.

That evening, as temple bells echoed in the distance and a boat glided across the glowing water, she leaned her head on Ayush's shoulder.

"I don't know what tomorrow holds," she whispered.

Ayush kissed her forehead softly, "We'll hold it together. That's enough."

And it was.

Because for the first time, Pranavi wasn't searching anymore. Not for signs, not for validation, not for something missing.

She had finally arrived — not at a destination, but at a pause. A sacred pause between chapters, where everything just… made sense.

The sky deepened into twilight. Somewhere nearby, a child laughed. An old priest lit diyas by the river. And the world continued to spin — imperfect, chaotic, beautiful.

As Pranavi watched the flame of a single diya float away into the night, she made no wish.

She simply whispered, "Thank you."

Thank you to the universe.

Thank you to the heartbreaks.

Thank you to the long lonely walks.

Thank you to the friends who stayed, and even to the ones who didn't.

Thank you... to herself.

For choosing to rise.

For daring to hope.

For learning that love is not a person, but a place within you — and when the time is right, someone simply walks in and finds home.

And now, a new story would begin.

But for now... she breathed.

And the river kept flowing.

To Be Continued...

Because the best stories never really end. They just find new places to begin again.

Epilogue

Ayush finds a scribbled note in her old diary:

"If love is a river, you were my ocean."

The Places I See Us

There are places I've never been to –
hidden cafés in the hills, narrow bylanes
lit by dying street lamps, forgotten temples
whispering old chants — and yet, I know
how it would feel to walk there... with him.

I imagine us together – not as tourists,
but as souls quietly reclaiming every corner
that once lived only in dreams.

I'd sit beside him on a moss-covered step,
watching the world drift by. He'd
speak of places he'd loved in solitude, and
I'd feel myself becoming one of them.
We wouldn't need pictures. Just our laughter
echoing off old bricks, our stories dancing
in temple bells and riverside winds.
Some love stories aren't about time or place.
They unfold in sacred corners of the mind,
where longing becomes poetry even in absence.

—P.

Author's Note

This story is a whisper of hope for anyone who's ever loved in silence, healed in private, or waited for something the world said was impossible. Thank you for letting Pranavi be a part of your heart.

About the Author

Pronami Borah is a storyteller at heart, a dreamer by soul, and an HR leader by profession. With over 15 years of experience in building people-first workplaces, she brings the same emotional depth and authenticity into her writing.

Born and raised in Assam, she writes from a place of reflection and quiet strength often drawing from her own journey through love, loss, and becoming. To the One Who Never Knew is her debut book - a deeply personal narrative inspired by real moments and unsaid emotions that lingered too long.

Beyond her professional and literary worlds, Pronami is also a passionate singer. Her soulful renditions - shared through singing videos are a creative outlet that mirror the same vulnerability and honesty found in her words.

When not working, writing, or recording music, she finds peace in journaling at sunrise, mentoring young professionals, or simply sipping chai while reminiscing about home.

Dedication

To everyone who has ever loved silently, lost without closure, and still chose to rise again.

And to the one who, unknowingly, taught me the quiet strength of letting go.

Acknowledgements

This book would not have been possible without the unwavering support of my family, friends, and readers - each of you have carried me through every page, every pause, and every moment of doubt.

To my mother and brother - thank you for being my world. Your love is the foundation of everything I am and everything I strive to be.

A heartfelt thank you to my dearest mentors and friends, Kanupriya and Poonam. You've been more than just guides - you've been my strength, my sounding boards, and my reminders of what I'm capable of. Your belief in me has helped me scale heights I never thought I could reach.

To Surabhi, Divya, and Aditi - though we may not talk every day, please know that each one of you hold a very special corner in my heart. Your silent support, laughter, and sisterhood have made the unbearable bearable. I carry your love like a warm memory, always.

And finally, to the one person who transformed my life by simply walking into it - you know who you are. Your presence has been my turning point. You've taught me the true essence of strength, patience, and hope. I will always cherish the light you've brought into my life.

To every silent supporter, every message of encouragement, every unspoken prayer, and every shared tear - this story belongs to you as much as it belongs to me.

With love and deep gratitude,

Pronami